If TWO ARE DEAD

"Three can keep a secret if two of them are dead."

-Benjamin Franklin

Merry Christmas

J. Arvid

OTHER BOOKS BY J. ARVID ELLISON:

Dangerous Fishing, 2011
Dangerous Blessing, 2012

IF TWO ARE DEAD

J. Arvid Ellison

TATE PUBLISHING
AND ENTERPRISES, LLC

Published by Tate Publishing & Enterprises, LLC
127 E. Trade Center Terrace | Mustang, Oklahoma 73064 USA
1.888.361.9473 | www.tatepublishing.com

Tate Publishing is committed to excellence in the publishing industry. The company reflects the philosophy established by the founders, based on Psalm 68:11,
"The Lord gave the word and great was the company of those who published it."

Book design copyright © 2013 by Tate Publishing, LLC. All rights reserved.
Cover design by Rodrigo Adolfo and Autumn Roberts
Interior design by Deborah Toling

Published in the United States of America
ISBN: 978-1-62510-403-8
1. Fiction / Thrillers / Military
2. Fiction / Romance / Suspense
13.09.20

DEDICATION

To my family and friends.

Emily Dickenson wrote, "My friends are my estate; forgive me the avarice to hoard them." It is because of my supporting family members and my great friends I am able to enjoy the encouragement that allows me to continue writing. Tate Publishing has been extremely helpful in its many departments; editorial, art layout and design, and marketing. They have become my friends as well. I couldn't ask for better. Special thanks go to Autumn Roberts for her manuscript suggestions and her submission of an intriguing cover design. A book is a work of many and sometimes only the author gets recognized.

CHAPTER 1

"Three can keep a secret if two of them are dead."
-Benjamin Franklin

Yells erupted spontaneously. Emphatic "yeses" and hearty "yeahs" spread throughout the cabin. Cheers rumbled on from there like thunder across the plains as the huge airplane rolled down the runway. Soldier arms stretched into the air; some had clinched fists shaken in triumph. The flight crew had smiles on their faces. The airplane carrying them to the mobilization station at Fort Carson Colorado bumped first on the wing wheels and then gently came down upon the nose wheel. Everyone needed to let out an exclamation of celebration. Their families were only few miles away waiting for them at the big post field house.

"We're home," Jerry spoke with quiet awe to his seatmate. Then he turned back around the edge of his aisle seat and stared at his friend Kathy sitting behind. He gave her a thumbs-up and spoke the words he thought she would appreciate. "You made it! I told you, didn't I?" Her smile appeared to be gratitude, yet something more.

Jerry and Kathy's small company was combined with other larger units returning from Afghanistan. Their mapping company had spent a year in theater working to provide a small but necessary element of warfare—accurate maps. They were the computer geeks who made the equipment run with fancy programs that translated on-the-moment satellite photos into topographical symbols easy to read in the field. They were mobilized reservists. Their term of service was drawing to a close, and they had only a week more of military requirements to endure. The freedom they fought for was now overshadowed by a different kind of freedom: freedom from first sergeants.

The bright, high-altitude sunlight of Colorado greeted them as they exited the plane, and they were also greeted by the commanding general of Fort Carson with his shiny stars reflecting the midday sun. He shook their hands, greeting each with a warm, "Job well done! Thank you!" It was nice to have a two-star general personally greet them, but anticipation in seeing wives, family, and girlfriends and boyfriends trumped that experience like miles over inches. As they walked to the processing building, they could see the busses waiting to drive them to the reception at the field house. They needed first to check in weapons, sign for their billet rooms, and get an "in-country" briefing from the rear detachment commander. While they stood in lines, there was a big-screen television broadcasting the scene at the reception site. Many soldiers stared at the screen, hoping to get a glimpse of their loved ones waiting in the stands. Jerry was at the front of most of the lines and got to the bleachers earlier than most. He watched the TV scan back and forth across the stands. He couldn't see Sharon. All deployment he longed for this moment, for this day, for the kiss and the embrace that would make the twelve months of dirt and dust disappear.

Kathy joined him in the stands as he watched. She was a petite sprite with a lot of spunk that allowed her to work in an almost-male environment. She could give back as much as she got. Her lustrous dark hair was pinned-up underneath her helmet, showing her delicate neck and emphasizing her light, smooth skin. She wore the web-gear like every other soldier, and it made her look heavier than she actually was. Her figure was lost in the pounds upon pounds of "Battle Rattle" she had to carry.

She was from the same unit as Jerry. They lived in South Dakota but in cities over a hundred miles apart. They had become close friends on the deployment because they worked in the same complex and in the same cubical farm. When her boyfriend back home had dropped her with one of those letters halfway through the mobilization, she needed to share with a friend her ripped-apart feelings. Jerry had been the ear for her to bend. Many evenings she would talk and he would listen. Secretly she wished he had not been in a serious relationship, because he had exhibited the characteristics her boyfriend lacked and everything she wanted in a man.

Jerry's blond hair did not poke out from beneath his helmet, because it was military short. His light sun-colored eyebrows did. Blue eyes strained to read faces and the characteristics of the crowd. He had in his pocket a moderately expensive diamond ring.

"Have you seen her yet?" Kathy asked.

"Not yet. I can see they're still coming in the doors. Y'know she's almost always late. She can't be late for this!" Jerry punctuated his words with worry.

"Have you got the ring ready?"

"In my pocket."

The big-screen TV snapped off. The commander of troops at the mob-station was ready to tell them of the things they needed to know about the present situation at Fort Carson and the Colorado Springs community. "Everyone's happy for you to come home safely…" *Yadda, yadda, yadda.* Anticipation translated the speech into nonsense. The words of the commander left their thoughts as fast as they entered their ears. "For a year now many of you have been saving a lot of money. Don't spend it all in one place. There are many car dealers willing to help you unload all your money on expensive cars and motorcycles..." *yadda, let us see our families, yadda, yadda.* "If any of your experiences from Afghanistan come back to you in the form of dreams..." *Yadda, yadda, we've heard this a hundred times, yadda.* "I won't keep you from your families..." *Yeah!* "...busses are through the doors on your left, my right..." *It's about time!*

The soldiers filed from the stands and through the doors. Kathy grabbed Jerry's hand and said, "I'm happy for you. Congratulations!"

"Thanks."

"Are you nervous?"

Jerry took a huge breath and blew it out semi-slowly. "Yep." Then because the line was slow, he asked her. "Is there anyone going to be there for you?"

"No. My folks can't make the trip because of their injuries from the car accident several years ago, and my brothers are all busy with their work. They said they'd have a family barbecue to celebrate when I finally get home. I'm good with that."

"I'm sorry no one will be here to welcome you. I'll bring Sharon over to meet you when we're done celebrating."

Her eyes went to the floor. "Yeah, okay." Kathy felt she didn't sound very upbeat for him. She added, "That would be nice, but make sure you have all your attention focused on her. I don't want her to have wrong thoughts about our friendship. She might get the wrong idea, okay?"

"I wouldn't have thought of that."

"Guys usually don't think of things like that."

Outside they formed up into one large unit, eight ranks deep and fifty soldiers wide. They marched in through three sets of double doors while music played, "I'm Proud To Be An American," and the packed field house cheered and clapped in ecstatic glee. Soldiers trained to keep their eyes straight ahead while marching but were still checking through peripheral vision the bleacher seats for recognizable faces. Banners were hung everywhere announcing love for particular soldiers by name. But the returning soldiers focused only on faces. The top-ranking NCO called them to a halt, turned them by command to face the crowd and the dignitaries, and then put them at parade rest. They were not to move a muscle, unless by his command, until dismissed. The cheering families continued their adulation, but with more pointing and identifying of particular soldiers. On the front row, a six-year-old girl in a church dress saw her daddy on the front rank. She burst from standing next to her mother and started to run to her father. He did the best he could to signal that she should go back to her mom. She hesitated. The two-star general standing close by said, "Go ahead, sweetheart." She ran and leapt into her daddy's arms.

The crowd noise continued for another couple of minutes and then the adjutant called for the playing of the national anthem. The father sent his daughter back to her mother while the NCO called the unit to attention, executed a right face, and then present arms. The crowd stood and covered their hearts, soldiers saluted, as the anthem was sung by a local artist. The words and music tasted sweeter on American soil. They were home, minutes away from a three-day pass and a week away from total demobilization, and return to normal life in their hometowns. All they had to do was listen to one more speech and the three days were theirs.

The word "dismissed" came so suddenly they could hardly believe it. The general was true to his word that he would not keep them long. The soldiers rushed into the crowd, and the melee of crushing hugs and passionate kisses began. With so many in attendance, it was difficult for some to find their own. Some had espied them in the stands, but when the rush started, they lost them. Jerry didn't know which way to go, right or left. He was closer to the left, so he started from the extreme edge of the building and systematically cased the stands to the right.

Reporters were sticking microphones in faces and trying to catch tender intimate moments. On-the-spot interviews were ongoing everywhere. The reporters left Jerry alone. One look could tell them he was searching. Kathy didn't search. She watched. She studied Jerry to see if his Sharon would show up.

"So how does it feel to be home, Sgt. Pelletier?" Kathy was startled by the reporter's question as he tilted the mic toward her face. He had read her name off of her uniform. She hadn't even noticed him coming her way with his cameraman.

"Wonderful! At the beginning of the tour it seemed like it would take forever, but toward the end it went by swiftly." Kathy thought her remark was stating the obvious.

"What's it like being in war as a woman? Were you nervous? Afraid?"

"Ah, well, after I was there for a couple of months it seemed like normal, maybe a little boring. I went to work every day. I did my job and came home."

"Did you see a lot of violent action?"

"Not much, I was in a convoy that came upon a roadside bomb. It happened to a Striker vehicle five behind us. We rushed to help the wounded. One died. He was a good friend. I felt anger…and sadness all at the same time."

"Do you consider yourself a hero?"

"No. The soldiers who saw combat—risked their lives—they're the heroes, like Corporal Shuster who was killed. He's a hero." Kathy remained in place as the reporter turned on his heels and walked off without even a "thank you." She immediately searched the area for Jerry. She found him standing near the doors, watching the entrance and the crowded floor at the same time. Kathy went to the snack section and struck up a conversation with a USO representative. She munched on a glazed donut and sipped from one of the free water bottles. She wanted to be far away from Jerry when Sharon showed up. The field house was emptying. Soldiers took the families out to the back, collected their bags that had been loaded off the trucks, and went to their cars. There wasn't a need to hang around. Jerry was confronted by a different reporter.

"So, how was your tour Sgt. Svenson?"

"Ah, fine I suppose." Jerry's eyes strayed away from the reporter as he kept his vigil of the floor area and the door.

"Did you see combat?"

"No, not unless you consider wrestling with a paper jam combat. Computer operations can be rugged."

"Were you nervous about being in such a violent environment?"

"No. It can be more risky here in the United States with all the people texting and driving at the same time."

"Now that you're home, what are your plans?"

Jerry looked frustrated. "My plans? My plan…I guess I'll execute *my plan* as soon as I get my chance." He turned his head and scanned the doors and the empting staging area.

"Thank you, Sgt. Svenson, welcome home." The reporter could see there was little else to do but go to the news van and file his report for the evening news.

"At least you got a 'thank you' and a 'welcome home.' All I got was the back of a shirt. No Sharon yet?" Kathy asked.

"No. I wonder where she is." Jerry's voice was far away.

"Call her. They have phones in the back set up so we can call anywhere in the US for free. I'm going to call my folks."

"Good idea."

A broad smile dominated Kathy's face. Her folks were happy she was home safe. They had praised her sacrifice for her country and said they were very proud of her. She hung up the phone with assurances there would be a big party in her honor after she got home. They didn't spoil the conversation with any references to the ongoing medical battles they were suffering. This talk was focused on her and her accomplishment. She looked for Jerry.

Jerry's shoulders drooped; his head was down. He politely ended his talk. After he hung up, Kathy could see he held the ring box in his hand. He dropped his hand, and the box brushed against his leg. It fell out of his hand onto the floor. He stared at it. It didn't take a counselor trained in body language to calculate what had happened. Kathy could read the entire story from his simple reaction. Without hesitation she went to him and stood silently by. He knew she was there but said nothing. She waited. After what seemed like an hour, she asked.

"What happened?"

"Sharon ended it."

"What did she say?"

"She didn't. She told my folks."

"Oh."

"I couldn't get her to answer her cell, so I called my folks. I figured, why not? The call is free. They told me she called them and didn't want to see me. You know what? I think they agreed with her." His head moved from one side to the other like it had been hit with a slow-motion right hook and a left jab.

"Agreed with her? Why?"

"You know they don't like me being in the army. Sharon told them she doesn't want to wait for me to get done playing soldier. They didn't say so, but I felt like they were waiting for me to finally see their argument against all war." Jerry bent to pick up the ring box. "Now all I have is this useless trinket! It has zero meaning for me now." His hand almost crushed the tiny gift box. He looked around with moist eyes. All his rosy plans, the beginning of his new future, his comfortable state of belonging, were lost in a four-minute talk with his folks. His sacrifice of a year out of his life for his country was overshadowed by a futile feeling of an empty American dream. "I need to get out of this place."

Kathy pointed him to where the personal gear and luggage had been stacked outside next to the truck. There were only a couple of piles left—one pile of battle gear on top of a single duffle bag for each soldier. They didn't have trouble locating theirs. They silently shouldered the bags and walked to the shuttle bus that would take them to the billets. Only a dozen soldiers out of the hundreds that had entered the field house needed transportation.

Still no words shared the space between them as they rode the five-minute trip to housing. Kathy let Jerry dwell in his cave of thought. When they got off the mini bus, she made a suggestion. "Jerry, I'm going to get settled, shower, and put on some jeans for the first time in months. Then I'm going to the all-night snack bar and stay there waiting for you."

"Why?"

"Remember how you talked to me when I was down? Well, I owe you."

"Ah, I don't know. I'll crash and try to sleep this off."

"Okay, I understand. But...I'll still be there until late if you need me. Remember the midnight mess hall at Camp Honor where you listened to me? You made me laugh again and feel normal. I don't have your sense of humor, but I'll do my best," Kathy said.

Jerry shuffled up the stairs to the third floor. Kathy's room was on the main level. True to her word, Kathy went to the snack bar and ordered a large burger and a plate of fries. She did this after buying a novel at the small PX in the same building. She settled in for a long evening, ready in case she could be the help that her dear friend needed. Whenever anyone entered, her eyes flew off the page to see if it was Jerry.

Two hours later a hollow man came through the door. The form-fitting jeans and the pullover gave a different look than the bulky combat mesh vest with all the pockets and pouches filled with soldier necessities. He had a good physique that showed despite his bent shoulders. Deployment was good for him. The exercise and weight training had added and tightened muscles.

He could easily serve as a shirtless male model. His hair was wet from a recent shower.

"Couldn't sleep." He slumped into the booth on the other side of the table.

"Almost all of us slept some on the plane. Your cycles are all messed up."

"Nah, that's not it. All I can think is 'what can I do to get her back?' I can quit the army. Maybe she'll reconsider. Wha'd'ya think?"

"I would ask her first if that would make a difference." Kathy wanted to say that the excuse Sharon used may not be the real reason, but she didn't want to launch Jerry into a world of 'what could it be?'

"Asking her is going to be a problem. She's not answering her phone."

"Are you going to get a cell phone? It might be better than standing in the hallway trying to talk to her with the payphone."

"I'll get a cell phone package at home with Wi-Fi, cable, and everything included. Besides I have all these prepaid phone cards to use up. If I get to talk, I should be able to cover at least four hours of conversation. I'd be happy with two minutes, just to hear her voice." Jerry looked down.

"I understand. I felt the same way." Kathy put her hand over Jerry's. "Tell me, what will you say to her if you get her on the phone?"

"That I'll do anything to get her back."

"Anything else?"

"I don't know."

"Tell her you miss her and love her," Kathy suggested. Jerry nodded his head.

"Should I tell her about the ring?"

"I think that might push the issue too much. You want her to love you for you. Not for what you can give her."

"Okay…" Jerry's voice traveled away. Kathy watched and listened as he tried other suggestions and desperate ideas. They stayed at the table until 2 a.m. It looked as if he would fall asleep from emotional exhaustion. Kathy suggested he get some sleep, and they went back to the barracks building. They missed breakfast in the morning and slept until late. Their body clocks were in the same foreign time zone.

The weekend and the final de-mob week sped by for Kathy and oozed in slow motion for Jerry. They completed their physicals and psychological tests and filled out paper work for every detail expected and unexpected. Jerry got his truck out of secure storage where it had stayed for the year. It raised his spirits a little to have wheels once again. They were given a choice of airfare or travel mileage and per diem to go home. Kathy elected travel mileage and per diem in the hopes that she could ride back to South Dakota with Jerry.

Jerry tried every phone number of every friend he knew Sharon had. The effort he put out was titanic. He knew she must know he was trying to contact her. It added to his dismal outlook on the prospects. He finally got a hold of Sharon's younger sister, Brenda, who was unaware of the controversy. Jerry didn't tell who he was. He acted as if he was from her work, needing to talk about schedules. Brenda said, "She's over at Bill's. She's always at Bill's. Do you want his number?"

He didn't want Bill's number. He knew who Bill was, but he asked for it anyway to stay in the guy-from-work persona. The history of Bill and Sharon went way back to junior high with their on-and-off relationship. Hopeful prospects were fading. Kathy now felt she could voice a suspicion she had carried most of the week.

"Jerry, I think Sharon is avoiding you because she feels guilty for being with someone else." Her words were the reality of the echoing fears he already had but could not accept. He went silent for a long time. Then Kathy made her request. "Jerry, would you drive me home? It's kinda on your way if you go north first instead of east." She held her breath, wondering if he was too depressed to want company on the drive. She didn't know how welcoming it was for him to not be alone.

"I would like that, but I'm not leaving right away."

"Oh, why?"

"You know I like taking pictures of wildlife. I want to take an extra day with my camera up in the mountains. Who knows when I will get another chance to be in Colorado? Besides, why am I rushing back?"

"You're a great photographer. I've seen your pictures. Can I come along?"

"Sure, I'll show you my pet mountain lion." Jerry smiled for the first time in days.

"The one you had a picture of that you pinned to the wall in your cubical?"

"Yep."

"Is he really friendly?" Kathy asked with disbelief.

Jerry chuckled at her question. "No way. I spent two hours watching him sun himself on a rock out-cropping. I plan on going there to see him again."

"That sounds exciting…and dangerous."

"It's only dangerous if you stay above timberline in the afternoon."

CHAPTER 2

He looked goofy wearing his cowboy hat off-center and over one ear. Both of his hands were shoved deep into the pockets of his shabby, soiled jeans. He didn't like being left behind to guard cars. He wanted to be a part of the action. The group commander of the small fragment of the Patriot Posse was laying down the law to his dumbest recruit. If Bradley were a clock, the hour hand would be missing. The commander had to leave very specific instructions.

"Bradley, this is a very important job. You must see to it that no one touches these cars or tries to get into them, especially my four-by-four, because it has the money in it. You are protecting our money for operations. Good people have donated it to support our cause. Do not take your eyes off of the money. Do you understand?" The commander's eyes bored into him like lasers.

"Yes, sir!" Bradley processed the information and answered with the preprogrammed response.

"I know you stole that car." He pointed at the yellow sports car. "It was a very stupid thing to do. We don't want to call any attention to ourselves. If anyone traces that car to you, we will not help you. We won't know you, and you won't know us, got it? You will be out of the Posse. Do you understand? Get rid of the car as soon as possible."

"Yes, sir!"

The commander started down the trail after the others, who had a five-minute head start. "We'll all be back in a couple of hours. And, Bradley, don't forget, eyes on the money, all the time."

He watched his commander disappear around the edge of a rock pile and then suddenly became bored. He fidgeted and kicked stones. He took the small revolver, a Walther PPK, out of his belt in the small of his back and aimed it at trees and rocks, making *thwet* sounds as if it had its silencer attached. Then he remembered the great stereo system in the car. He went to the car and sat in the front seat, turned on the sound system, completely reclined the driver's seat, and lay back to listen. It took several minutes to realize he had neglected to watch the money. He bolted straight up and went to the black SUV to see if the bag was still there. He was torn between "eyes on" and great music. Slowly the idea dawned upon him. He took the tote bag and put it in the back of the Camero and settled into the seat to lose himself in the beats and rhythms.

Twenty minutes later he saw a silver pickup traversing the winding road as it doubled back on itself and climbed up to his location. He switched off the stereo and slunk down in the seat to hide.

They had signed out of the unit at 0900 with their terminal leave papers in neat folders. A full army breakfast sat in their stomachs, yet they drove to the nearest Quiznos restaurant to buy foot-long sandwiches. They would need them for the hiking through rugged terrain and waiting for animals to appear.

When they got to the trailhead, it already contained several cars. There wasn't room for his truck in the small parking lot, so he turned the truck around and parked it on the verge of the road behind a yellow Camero.

"I've never known this place to be so popular. I hope they haven't spooked the big cat away," Jerry wished out loud. Both of the hikers had small daypacks with the basic essentials of sun-screen, rain gear, water, a thin blanket, and first aid supplies. Like well-trained soldiers, they checked each other's pack and tightened and tied all straps to cut down on noise.

They entered the same trail the commander had taken. After a good hike down the trail, Jerry climbed a boulder pile and glassed ahead with his binoculars. He handed them to Kathy and quietly pointed out the rock shelf the puma had sunned on a year before. She silently acknowledged the spot, and they went into a stealthier mode. They had another mile to go off trail, through uneven terrain with piñon pines and lichen-covered rocks to slow their travel. Jerry clicked many photographs of unique flora and grand vistas of the Great Plains. He was in his element. When he snapped a particularly nice shot, he let Kathy see it on the view screen. Always she smiled and nodded her approval. They moved on to an over-watch position with a clear view of the cat's sunny patio. They settled into comfortable positions to wait.

No mountain lion was visible. The answer why came to their ears. Voices and the sound of shovels hitting rocks came to their attention. It was nearby. With the presence of humans close, no puma in his right mind would linger. Jerry and Kathy walked over to the ledge and looked down. Below the overhang and less than a hundred yards away, a cluster of men were digging and watching. Two were down in the hole, and three were above. Several file-folder-sized boxes were stacked by the hole. It was obvious they were going to bury the boxes.

Jerry and Kathy looked at each other quizzically. When one of the men started to look around the perimeter, the soldiers ducked simultaneously. The men were nervous and alert. Jerry saw a sentinel back up toward where the group had left the trail. Looking the other way, he found another sentinel was on a rock directly opposite. Jerry assumed the prone position, and Kathy followed suit.

"They're doing something illegal," he whispered. He snapped a couple of pictures and switched his camera to video mode.

Because Jerry had taken them on a circular route to the overhang, their presence was unknown by the seven men. They watched with interest and listened. Jerry held his camera, Kathy watched through the binoculars. It looked as if the man in the brown long-sleeve shirt was in charge. He directed one of the diggers to get out of the hole, and then he started a speech partially audible to the pair. When his back was to them, they heard mumbling. When he turned partially their way, they could hear better. The man leaned down and opened a box and took out a sheet of paper.

"...see what's in.... This is...tant...isn't..." Then he walked around to the opposite side of the hole and squatted down to look straight into the eyes of the man still holding the shovel. "I think you know what this is. Here, take a look. Recognize it? It's a transcript of your cell phone calls for the last month. Look at the numbers circled in red." The individual in the hole suddenly looked up from the paper; his body tensed. He started to climb out of the hole. "Stay where you are! That number you called so often is the handler for your undercover operation. You can see why we need to bury this paper deep and in a place far from public scrutiny. Oh, and we need you to be buried with it."

"Wait, if you kill me, my agent will turn you in."

"Not any more he won't. We took care of him last night." The agent in the hole swung his shovel in a futile attempt to hit the man in the brown shirt. Two pistols began firing, and the leader stood up and drew his gun and added the *coup de gras*.

Kathy inhaled sharply and looked at Jerry in distress. He held the camera on the scene. He had captured the whole execution. He held the camera for two more beats of his racing heart and then whispered, "We've got to get out of here, and fast!"

They slunk back to the bushes. They helped each other to stuff the camera and the binoculars in their packs and then moved quickly through the brush. Jerry kept an eye on the general area where the sentinels were. He would not allow them the advantage of seeing their escape. They circled out wider than the route they had come. Jerry wondered why the guards had not seen them. When they finally got to the trail, they ran uphill. The sound of their feet on loose rocks and gravel alerted the one guard. The pursuit was on. Jerry hoped they had at least enough lead on the killers, if they had discovered their presence.

Out of breath and almost to the point of muscle cramps, they crested the hill and surprised a befuddled man standing in from of them. They had a moment of confusion. Jerry took Kathy's arm and casually moved toward his truck, removing the keys from his pocket.

"Wait a minute." He pulled his gun out of the small of his back. "I want that pickup!" Jerry and Kathy froze. "You heard me. Give me the keys." Their lack of movement matched their lack of understanding. They now had no means of escape except running into the trees. Then Bradley surprised them. "Take the Camero, the keys are in it."

Their heads swiveled back and forth. They were being forced to steal a car, the owner was offering his and stealing theirs. A cell phone rang in Bradley's pocket. He wasn't good at multitasking.

"Go, stupid people! Go!"

"Hello? …Hello? I can't hear you. Can you hear me? …Hello?"

They shuffled nervously toward the Camero. They wanted to go and go quickly. They wanted to stay because they didn't want to lose the truck. They didn't want to be caught by the murderers, so they wanted to go. Their feet were making the decision for them. They kept their eyes on the strange fellow barking into his phone who then fired into the ground at their feet. Jerry and Kathy bolted toward the Camero, and Jerry threw his keys in the general direction of his pick-up.

Laughter followed the couple as they fumbled to jump in the car. Jerry watched as he started the car, hunched up and clinging to the steering wheel with the seat down in the fully reclined position and then bent over with glee. He watched as the man hit callback on his cell, trying to make a better connection. He stomped his foot in disgust and watched the Camero as it burned away from the parking lot. Jerry kept tabs on the man through the rear window as the man's hands went to his head, and his body swiveled to look at the black SUV and then back at them. He saw the man slam the phone on the ground and the pieces fly in different directions. Then he stomped his feet again and again in a circle of anger then bent to pick up the pieces of the phone.

Jerry was doing his best to drive and hang on to the wheel for support. "I don't understand, why would he steal our truck and make us take his car! 'Cause it has a broken seat? Why?" Kathy was coming out of her shock.

"Jerry, maybe this car's stolen too. He's dumping one that's hot for one that's not so hot."

Humor was the last thing Jerry needed now but he couldn't leave the line just sitting there unused. "What'cha mean my truck's not so hot?"

"You can joke at a time like *this*?"

"Why not? It's better than screaming until my head pops off." Kathy smiled and Jerry smirked. He concentrated on the road. The tension dropped a single notch, just enough to help Kathy focus. She saw the bow to his back and the sway his body made as he clung to the wheel he was turning. She crawled over the center console and put her hand down the side of the driver's seat. She found the lever and raised the seat; it slowly squeezed her between the rising seat and Jerry's back. Her face pressed into the middle of his back.

"Easy, girl, not now. I'm a little busy." Kathy squeezed herself out of the vortex with a hand on his side. The temptation to pinch him was difficult to stifle. "When we get down off this mountain, we'll drive straight to the police and report everything we saw," Jerry added.

"Okay, but if this is a stolen car, then we might never get to the police station. We'll be picked up as car thieves."

"Right, I hadn't thought of that. We'll keep off the main roads and walk the last couple of blocks," Jerry corrected. Kathy had looked back to see if they were being followed.

"Jerry they're coming after us. It looks like they're driving your truck."

"The not-so-hot truck?"

"Yeah, that one. What are we going to do?" she asked.

"Is it that idiot? And, *is* he alone?"

"Can't tell. He's pretty far back but coming fast, very fast! Step on it!" Kathy ordered.

"Maybe he's just being nice and wanting to return our luggage we left in the truck," Jerry quipped.

"Not likely, he shot at us!" Kathy exclaimed.

"You've got a point." Jerry added more speed and doubled back and forth across the face of the mountain. Kathy kept a watch on the road above them. She gasped as she saw the pickup charge off the road and straight at them.

"Jerry! He's coming straight down the mountain!"

Jerry could not resist looking at his truck crashing over the rough terrain. It flew through the air and smashed into rocks slewing sideways and almost rolling. Kathy saw the front bumper crushed by rocks under the grill and then get run over by the wheels. Next the hood sprang up and obscured the windshield, blocking the driver's view. One of her suitcases carved a beautiful arc against the blue sky. When it landed, it burst open in an array of dresses, uniforms, and cosmetics. The spare tire dislodged from hanging behind the rear axle. It bounced into the air and wobbled its own path down the mountain. One side panel had a ragged hole in it where a piece of dead wood had speared the truck when it had careened sideways.

Jerry could tell that the shortcut helped the pursuer gain on them, haphazard as it was. He stepped on it only to have to slow down drastically for the next hairpin turn cutting back along the mountain. He approached the point of convergence where the car would meet the truck. He wanted to get ahead before the truck passed in front but couldn't make it. He stopped to watch as the out-of-control truck bucked its way across the road in front of them. The driver looked like a rag doll being thrashed about. The truck proceeded over the berm, leaving the smoking sizzling muffler on the edge of the road. The truck gained more speed on the steep hill. The next switchback brought them back toward the falling truck. It slammed down on the road and rolled up against the tree. One deflated tire hung in the air spinning. The back bumper was bent and hanging by one bolt. Smoke began to pour out of the engine compartment. Jerry didn't slow down.

"Okay, okay. It's not so hot." As they approached, fire began flickering out of the front wheel well. "Then again, maybe not." Jerry's eyebrows arched.

✺✺✺

A battered and bloodied Bradley kicked the door open and slithered out of the truck. He yelled at them, "Give me the money!" as the Camero shot by. He reached for his gun in his belt in back, and found it had slid down in his underwear. He groped around and finally had to retrieve it by reaching down the front of his pants. He staggered forward to the point where he could fire at the Camero as it passed beneath him on the lower road. He fired round after round at the speeding sports car. Slumping to the ground in the middle of the road, he took stock of his circumstances. He needed to return his commander's call. He reassembled the phone from the pieces in his pocket. The cell phone vibrated immediately in his hands when he turned it back on.

✺✺✺

Commander Webber received the call on his cell phone from the sentinel and swore. He immediately called Bradley, but got nothing. Then he heard the single report of a small-caliber weapon. His men were almost finished hiding signs of the grave. Two gathered the empty boxes used to fool the informant into thinking they were burying evidence, and the others were spreading pine needles over the site to hide the freshly turned earth. Webber wanted to break something, anything. He phoned Bradley repeatedly as they trekked back to the cars. It took several calls before Bradley answered. Commander Webber and his men were almost back to the parking lot when he finally got through.

"Where are you? Why didn't you answer? ...Why didn't you tell us there were people in the area? ...What? ...You're where?" The Commander could have melted rocks in his mouth. Bradley was spinning a wild tale of two people stealing the Camero. "At least the money is safe... They have that *too*? How? ...You idiot! You stupid id—Where are they now?" When he got the answer, the commander clicked off and immediately called a police dispatcher. His voice became smooth and businesslike. "This is Lieutenant Webber. I've located a stolen vehicle. Please send patrol cars to the entrance of Forest Road 332. A late-model yellow Camero is traveling northwest on that road right now. Thank you. I'm in pursuit in my personal vehicle with friends."

The collection of posse members was from different professions. They were sworn to secrecy and determined to stand in the place of municipal police departments when the federal, and by consequence state governments, would fail. They believed that would be soon. They solicited private funds for organizational purposes in untraceable currency—cash and bonds. They trained regularly. Until the government would fail, or was close to failing, they had to keep their vigilante activity out of public view. With their diverse support, they were able to tap almost unlimited resources legitimately for their clandestine activities. Commander Webber worked for the police department and used their surveillance capabilities. He was using his clout now to capture two car thieves, which served his covert agenda. It didn't matter what they said when they were caught. Nobody would believe them.

"Did he say…money?"

"That's what I thought he said. Why would he say that?" Kathy responded. She shook her head, and then curiosity drove her to look in the back seat. Behind the driver's seat on the bench seat was a large tote bag big enough to carry hockey gear. It was bulging. Kathy launched herself between the seats and unzipped the bag partway. In an instant she added another complication to their dangerous situation. The numbskull who had forced them to take his stolen car had failed to take out his stolen loot. "There's money back here!"

"Really?"

"Really. Um, Jerry, we not only have a hot car, but some hot money as well. If we get caught with this, the police will never believe our story!"

"We'll just have to get to the police station before the police get to us." They drove into heavier wooded country. The pine trees were taller Douglas firs and some aspen trees were mixed in on the sunnier slopes. Jerry kept his eye on the ground way out ahead. Whenever he could see down into the valley through breaks in the forest, he slowed to capture a better of view of any activity they might run into.

"Just curious, how much money is it?"

"A lot. It's a big bag with bundles tossed in."

"Are the bundles wrapped in paper strips? The strips might tell us which bank they came from."

Kathy reached back and pulled a large bundle into her lap. It was bound in a thick rubber band. The bills were mostly hundreds with a few fifties, twenties, and smaller denominations mixed in. Some were old, faded, and tattered. Others were pristine new. "I don't think these are from a bank. I don't know for sure, but this doesn't look like a bank heist." Jerry didn't answer. He slammed on the brakes and slid to a stop behind a copse of aspen. Kathy hit the dashboard, and the money lodged in the front window. "What did you see?"

"I thought I saw a police car with its lights on." Jerry stared down the hill. "There! Did you see that? It's a police car going toward the entrance to this road."

"What are we going to do?"

"Hoof it." Jerry slammed the car in reverse and drove the car uphill to a thicker grove of pines. He jockeyed it between some trees almost out of sight. Then he shut off the engine. They got out and debated which way to go. Jerry had another debate going on in his head. He reached into the front window, took out the bundle of money, and opened the back door. The satchel of cash was heavy. He zipped up the top after putting the loose bundle back in and then looped the two handles over his shoulders like an army duffle bag. Kathy stared at him in disbelief.

"Why?" she questioned, as much with her facial expression as with her words.

"I'm thinking this money needs to get to the police. If we bring it into the station ourselves, it will strengthen our story and our degree of honesty. Also, I don't want the guys behind us to get to it first."

"Okay, then let's go. Which way?"

"In that direction is the nearest town. We'll go up and over this ridge." Carefully they walked over the road, stepping on hard-packed dirt and stones so as not to leave footprints in the dust. On the other side, they went under a large fir and walked on a thick blanket of pine needles. Dashing across a brush-covered field, they moved into a dense forest that carpeted the rocky ridge up to the jagged pine pointed skyline. It didn't take but a half mile for Jerry to break sweat. Kathy saw it.

"Jerry, stop. Let me help. That bag has to be heavy." As soon as he did, she started to take the bag off.

"No, you can't carry it, it's really very heavy." She felt the weight when she pulled it off. She knew she wouldn't be able to carry it more than a hundred yards.

"All right then, let me carry the two day packs. That should help a little." Jerry didn't protest his battle buddy's offer to help. They rested some more and then made the climb up the face of the ridge. They stopped again at a jumble of lichen-covered boulders amongst tall Blues Spruce. Jerry climbed one boulder behind a tree to observe below. Six vehicles matching the ones at the trailhead were lined up on the road where the Camero lay partially hidden. Not a single police cruiser was there.

Jerry asked for the field glasses, and Kathy handed them up. While he scanned, she was transferring several bundles of cash into her pack. Jerry wondered what happened to the cruiser until he saw it come up the hill without its emergency lights. His eyes lingered on the scene. The leader in the long-sleeve brown shirt approached the cruiser. The policeman got out and shook hands with the man. They stepped over to the Camero and examined it. The officer compared the license number to a folded paper he took out of his pocket. Then he started to scan the perimeter. Jerry lowered the glasses to keep reflections from revealing his position. Suddenly the group of men started to fan out in various directions, scanning the ground for tracks.

He watched. Some brushed away twigs and leaves. Others bent over and pulled back low-hanging branches. The circle widened. Then one man saw something on the route they had taken. Jerry tensed. The men and the officer clustered around the mark, and the officer held both arms in a V pointing up the ridge. Jerry could plainly see they were directly within the vector the officer pointed out. The officer keyed the walkie-talkie clipped to his shoulder and called in a status report.

Jerry jumped down off the rock to find Kathy loaded up with both packs strapped to her back. He looped the bag handles over his shoulders, but before he could move, Kathy took the binoculars off of his neck and put them on hers. Jerry took the same route up with a slight angle to the right. When they topped the ridge, he asked Kathy to stay where she was. He then made several heavy steps down the hill in the same direction, embedding his heels deep into the soft soil until he had gotten to a fallen log. Then he backtracked using his same footsteps until he reached Kathy.

Carefully they worked their way up the ridge to the left in the direction of the trailhead they had left. Jerry was choosing a route most desperate people would not take. The straps bit into his shoulders, and his legs strained to keep pace.

Commander Webber rehearsed the story with his men that they would give the officer when Webber would call the policeman up from the roadblock.

"We saw the Camero driving away from the trailhead parking lot, and it matched the description of the stolen vehicle, okay? I called it in. We found a wrecked truck back up on the road. We think it belongs to one of the perpetrators, not sure. They may have wrecked the truck and needed another mode of transportation. They must have tried to come back to get their gear, or something. Say, 'We're just guessing at this point.' We think they're armed because we heard shots. Everyone got it? It's a simple story with ambiguity mixed in. Okay? I'm going to call them up to our position. Be willing to volunteer your services to help with the search." Webber made his call.

Bradley was banged up and sitting in the back seat of the SUV. He had given his description of the two to the others. Commander Webber didn't want him involved in the mix, and he only wanted his men to know the descriptions. It gave them the advantage over the police. Bradley was worried and angry at himself and at the two people he had forced to steal the Camero. He tried to please his commander by getting rid of the Camero but screwed up with the bag of donated money. He wanted to find them and kill them after he got back the money. It was the only way to get redemption.

Officer Webber was the competent professional as he greeted the officer from an adjacent town. They had met before in service meetings. When he explained the circumstances, the officer understood immediately. He checked the license number against a computer printout he made while waiting at the roadblock. He called in backup and initiated a manhunt. He called units from nearby communities to converge on his location where he was establishing a command post. His newly deputized volunteers were told to locate but not confront. The police would make the arrest. Then he had them fan out to look for tracks or signs of passage. It took five minutes to establish proof of direction and then he sent them out on a wide vector, hoping to drive the perpetrators down to the highway where he would establish a cordon.

They climbed higher and higher. Afternoon warmth added to the discomfort of traveling heavy. Always they tried to walk on bare rocks and dead logs to hide their spoor. Briefly Jerry stopped to check to see if there were signs of them being followed. They had established a large lead to begin with, and now, speed and direction was their best defense.

He marveled at Kathy's stamina. She never gave up, never faltered, and never suggested a rest stop. He could see the sweat drop from her neat, delicately curved eyebrows. The hair on her neck curled with the moisture. He didn't know if there was a village or a town in this direction, but he was sure that every policeman was alert to their flight. He needed to find a sizable town where the police would let them walk into the station unchallenged.

One hour, then two went by. He mused, *If we trained at this altitude, our troops would be in better shape.* The fright and flight of the morning had taken away all sensation of hunger. His nerves were a jumble, and his mind was a hodgepodge of facts. When he decided to let the police figure it out for him, he relaxed. Then a hunger pang jolted his senses.

"I'm hungry," he said in surprise.

"Hungry? How can you be hungry at a time like this?" Kathy's thoughts had been wrapped around worry and fear more than causes and whys. Her feelings were screaming for release from the trouble they were experiencing.

"We haven't eaten since this morning—that's more than six hours ago. We need to keep our strength up," Jerry instructed. Kathy agreed. They found a secluded cleft in the ridge of rocks. They were far above and west of the original trailhead where everything had cascaded upon them. Kathy opened one of her two packs to get out the sandwiches and chips. Jerry saw some of the bundles of money. "So…you plan on doing a little shopping later this evening?" She was too tired to make a snappy comeback. She gave him her amused smile and gently brushed his arm. "Thanks for being a great team mate," he said. They unrolled the subs and took bites.

She chewed and swallowed and then remarked, "I *am* hungry! I didn't realize it." She took a much larger bite.

"I'm thinking that I'll only eat half and save the rest for later," Jerry planned out loud. "And the water, we need to conserve what we have until we get more. What do you think?"

"Good thinking." They quietly ate and chewed slowly so the first bites would alert their systems to the presence of food and shut down the "hungerstat."

"Jerry, you know all those briefings on battle fatigue we had to sit through? You know, PTSD?"

"Yes."

"Well, I understand it better now. All I can see in my mind is the poor guy in the hole getting shot in the back. It keeps playing in my mind over and over. It's terrible! How about you?"

"Yes, sorta. I see it and I want to block it out of my mind. I switch over to what we have to do to survive," Jerry explained.

"Does that work for you?"

"A little. I'm wondering who those guys are and why someone had to work undercover to stop them. He was an innocent man working to protect us. I'm wishing I never brought you up here and got you into this mess."

"You didn't know this would happen. Neither did I."

"Yeah."

"We lost all our things."

"That, too," Jerry sounded resigned.

"You lost your ring."

"No, I have it. See." Jerry pulled a chain out of his shirt; the ring was on the chain around his neck.

"I thought it was in your bags."

"Last week I put it around my neck. I was hoping it would give me good luck and that she would change her mind. Stupid I guess."

"No, not stupid...sweet. You still love her."

"I guess, maybe, but it's hard to feel it when you're all messed up inside. And then, with all of this!" He waved his arm around, indicating their predicament.

They each took a small swig of water and began to gear up. They began their trek around the edge of the mountain. The ridge had played out. And they wanted to stay in the tree line. They moved for another two hours. Suddenly lightning struck nearby. They had not been paying attention to the high-altitude clouds. They trotted the best they could with the heavy loads.

"This is good," Jerry said.

"Why? I thought it was the last thing we needed."

"If it rains hard enough, it may wash away any signs we may have inadvertently left behind. The signs we left before the rain, but not the muddy prints after the rain. Let's go!" They ran as best they could. Later they had to break cover and dash across a field of brush, boulders, and windblown pines gnarled and misshaped like giant versions of Bonsai centerpieces.

Just past halfway across the open area, a bolt of lightning struck a dwarf tree ten yards away. The concussion of splitting air radiating outward blasted Jerry and Kathy off their feet and into a clutter of rocks. Jerry landed on his back with the tote bag cushioning his fall. Kathy smashed into the stones, scraping her arms and shins. Their ears rang as if artillery rounds had exploded close by. They clapped hands over their ears, but it didn't work because the ringing was coming from the inside.

Blood dripped down both of Kathy's forearms. Her jeans were scraped open on one knee. Jerry could see she was in pain and needed help. The wind picked up to a howl. She knew and he knew they had to get out of sight. He stood and took her hand, helping her up. Then they hobbled to the tree line, leaving a dislodged water bottle lying on the ground.

There were several rocks in a pile covered on one side with a low-growing juniper that filled the gaps between the stones. Underneath the thick spray of branches with prickly needles and hard bluish-green berry cones, existed a refuge with a deep carpet of forest refuse, old decaying aspen leaves, and tiny sharp bristles.

With a quick inspection, Jerry could see a sanctuary underneath. Animals had had the same idea and padded down the natural rubbish here and there. He guided her into the shelter that partially blocked the wind. They scooted around until their bodies fit the tight space. Then the rain began. The large tote bag was placed at her back for support and protection from the briarlike needles. Jerry searched for the first-aid kit. It had some wipes, which he used on her arms, and then he dressed the scrapes.

While he worked, her focus was not on her injuries. She soaked in the tenderness he exhibited and had a deep wish she could thank him with her lips. Next he folded her pant legs up and repeated his tender mercies to her shins and knee. Several of the dressing papers swirled around in the wind. After the first few got away, he was more careful. The rain began to soak their clothing. They had light rain gear and one poncho. Jerry tied the poncho's ends onto the juniper branches in a makeshift tent. He had one thin thermal army blanket that he wrapped around them both. "We're going to have to stay the night here." After a day of terror, a night in his arms was welcome. Their talk was covered by the sounds of the thunderstorm.

The unofficial Patriot Posse was officially tasked with herding the car thieves toward the highway. Two more officers with bulletproof vests walked with the group as it spread out in a wide fan, forcing the runaways on toward the road and the open fields where visibility was crucial to detection. Officer Webber walked in the middle, the other two on the fringe that expanded wider and wider as they moved forward. When the party crested the hill, they found Jerry's tracks leading downward. It gave them confirmation of direction. They didn't have to change their vector but a few degrees to one side. They were not thinking that the subjects of pursuit were using deception.

The day wore on as the search pushed to the edge of the wooded areas. Other police cruisers had stationed themselves in secluded vantage points, glassing the open areas. Nobody on foot crossed their vision. They radioed constantly to the searchers who were turned back to search for tracks. They returned to the last spot where they had seen tracks and split up into small groups going up and down the ridge to find any indications of human tracks. They had lost the direction of their escapees, and a thunderstorm was brewing. Officer Webber went with the other officer up to the truck and investigated. Immediately he called forensics to investigate a possible link to a crime.

Bradley accepted a ride from one of the other posse members and went to his small apartment. He cleaned and loaded his gun, grabbed an old pair of binoculars, and planned to return to the mountain and sit as high up as possible and watch after he got some sleep. He arose at 3 a.m., and rode his dirt bike back to the trailhead and took the mountain trail in the opposite direction and climbed upward. He broke out above the tree line at twelve thousand feet and sat watching the area where the road switched back and forth. He was on the other side of the mountain from where Kathy and Jerry had slept.

CHAPTER 3

High-altitude rain and wind brought temperatures down to uncomfortable levels. They spooned in an effort to share body heat. It wasn't freezing, but it felt like it. They tried to sleep but couldn't, so they talked. Each gave their own theory of what was going on. They concluded that the leader of the killers had some connection with the police because the police readily accepted him and his fellow killers in the manhunt. They also agreed that the lone person at the parking lot could also be connected. Their only hope was to get to a police department far enough away that would not instantly identify them as car thieves. Police in this vicinity were following a fabricated fairy-tale, and they were the evil ogres.

Physical and emotional exhaustion compelled them to sleep, and they awoke individually at around 4 a.m. Kathy awoke first, but remained completely still. She had daydreamed before of how it would feel to have his arms around her, now it was a reality; a reality forced upon them by a disaster not of their own making. He awoke twenty minutes later and stretched.

"It sounded like you slept well," Kathy spoke first.

"You're already awake? You didn't get up?"

"Do you think I'd give up a perfectly good heater?"

"You're right. It's still cold." He looked at his watch. "We should get going and put some more miles between us and them. How are you feeling?"

"Okay, I guess." They gathered their equipment. It was then they discovered the lost water bottle. They now had only three half-liter bottles, and they couldn't waste time searching for the lost one. They packed everything away, except the sandwiches, and started to walk. They ate as they moved. Travel was easier above timberline, but they needed to move downward to get to some water. More trees meant more obstacles. The going was slow. The sky lightened in the east, and visibility made it easier to find open ground. In the early-morning haze a thin smoke trail arose from beyond the ridge. It could be a campfire or perhaps a house furnace. They decided to move in that direction. The valley in between had to have a creek.

Bradley watched the sun come up. As the landscape detail materialized before his eyes, he started to chastise himself. *You stupid idiot! They wouldn't stay in the same area. They'd get as far away as possible. Maybe they'd go that way.* He rose and walked around the mountain on the tundralike landscape to see the other side of the mountain. He stopped at a high vantage point and started to glass the open areas. He spotted a herd of mountain goats grazing, and he watched them for a while. He turned his glasses away and then suddenly back to one goat, which was crushing a plastic water bottle in his mouth. In his mind it was hopeless to sit and watch a mountainside when the couple could have gone in any direction. He left his vantage point and wandered down to the mountain goats. He was a hunter and was drawn to wild game. The herd skittered away, and he found the masticated bottle. The paper label looked new, even with the teeth marks. On the label it read, "*Compliments of the USO, Fort Carson Colorado.*" This was more than Bradley could have hoped.

He found a freshly broken branch and then some blood drops on rocks. A trail was leading away to the west. Later, he saw the little papers from the bandages. Even a primitive man can follow this trail. Looking under the juniper bush where the papers had been stuck, he could see where they had slept. Having spent a great deal of time hunting, he knew this was fresh sign. He was so proud of himself he leapt and danced. *I'm not as stupid as people think, ha!*

He continued in the direction of the markings, from the bottle to the branch to the bivouac. He half ran for a mile and stopped because he had detected no sign. He went straight up the hill to find another lookout and watched for movement or color in the open areas with his binoculars. He waited for an hour and a half before he saw them rush across a forest road.

Going downhill made it easier with their loads. They followed a depression that kept them from being visible. They stayed in the trees, too, putting miles behind them. When they came to a road, they rested and gathered water in the rivulet running down the ravine. They were ever watchful for movement or noise. Then, like combat soldiers, they made a hasty rush through the open space and did not pause on the other side. They raced right up the hill as far as their strength could carry them. Then they picked their way through the forest on an azimuth toward their chosen objective. Even though they were accustomed to road marches and "movement to contact" training actions, as soldiers called them, they felt the burden and the strain. Their lives depended on it. A day later the horror of the ordeal was becoming manageable in their minds.

Sometimes Jerry led, sometimes Kathy. Each knew the objective. They neither spoke nor whispered. Each was winning the mental battle that fought to make them stop, slow down, or quit. They switched leadership so no one drove the other beyond their limit. Several hills and a ridge later, they looked down upon a campsite where the fire had been. They watched as kids played and ran around amongst the trees. They rested and then decided to go down and get some potable water from the pump in the campground instead of what they had gathered from the tiny source.

They stopped and fell to their bellies when a police cruiser drove in the entrance. They watched. Was it a routine patrol or not? It seemed out of place for a black-and-white to be in a forest campground instead of a forest ranger. The cruiser went to each of the campsites and delivered a message. Heads were nodding in agreement. Two families began to pack up and leave. Jerry and Kathy edged carefully away from the campsite and continued heading west.

Bradley watched intently the forest above the road for sign of movement amongst the trees. He was surprised to see a shadow flit upward on the hill. *They're moving fast*, he said to himself. He was sure when they crossed the road, one had a black tote bag on his back. It had to be them, with the money. He had a dilemma. They were too far to follow and catch. He studied where they were headed, and because he knew this country, he decided to return to his dirt bike and take the faster roads. He ran across the mountain in a straight line to the parking lot.

Jerry sat on a fallen log. He was familiar with where he had been before, but now they were moving onto unknown ground. He closed his eyes and relaxed. Kathy thought he was at his limit. She moved closer. "Need a rest? You look like you're tired."

"No, I'm just trying to visualize a map." He kept his eyes closed and breathed slowly and deep. From experience he knew if he concentrated hard he would be less successful in putting something together. Relaxed, he knew his mind could work freely. Map details were his forte. Terrain features on paper transposed into realism in a snap. He just had to remember. He pictured himself at his truck a year ago; the map spread out on the hood, his fingers tracing the roads, watercourses, and ridges. Another breath of fresh air and he could see it—a road weaving through a valley to a town called Bailey. They were in the Lost Creek Wilderness north of the Tarryall Mountains at altitude. The broad strokes of the map were clear, but the rugged little features weren't open to his memory. They had to move north; through what, he did not know. Drinking more water helped restore fluids lost in exertion. They kept going into the afternoon and evening. Jerry explained what he had been able to remember. His hope was for a town oblivious to their plight. Kathy's bandages rubbed against her jeans, and the adhesives gave up their properties. Several fell out of her pant leg, and blood started to ooze once again.

A large weather front caused the sunny sky to disappear. Thick clouds marched over the mountains to the west and settled into lower areas. These were not thunderstorms. A quick change of temperature alerted the two to colder thirty-degree air. The breeze added a bit more chill. If they kept going hard, their bodies would stay warm. They must get down out off high ground because rainy weather in early summer could translate to snow at ten thousand feet. High ground normally gave them an advantage in movement with less brush and more visibility. Visibility exposed them to prying eyes from further away. A straight line to Bailey took them up and down creating a change in speed; slow in the forests over fallen logs and dense undergrowth, fast at higher more treeless areas.

Night was coming early. Big fluffy flakes drifted across the fields, clinging to sage and spruce. The wind picked up, and the snow grew thick. They were in a gentle ascent up another ridge, wishing the opposite were true. Jerry was blind reckoning the direction toward Bailey. With the storm he now set his sight on closer landmarks so as not to wander in a circle. The tall grass was collecting its share of flakes, turning the ground into, at first, gray-green and then all white. They looked back and saw a clear trail where their feet had trod. All they could do was hope they were not being followed. It would take someone with the IQ of a donut not to be able to track them.

They crested the high ridge and descended to the valley floor. A barbed-wire fence blocked the way. Jerry held the top strand up and used his foot to push down the lower one. Kathy got through and returned the favor after Jerry took the bag off his back. They couldn't stand without freezing, so they moved on. The fence edged a field and gave them hope they were nearing civilization. In the darkness and with everything covered in snow, bushes looked like rocks, and large rocks looked like cars covered in white tarps. They came to a narrow lump that turned out to be a buffalo. They didn't know it until it moved. Others moved, too. They had walked into a rancher's herd. Their sudden human appearance startled the animals to bolt and run. They rumbled straight at the soldiers, who didn't know which way to go.

Twin sounds of wet mud under the snow and pounding thunder assaulted their senses. They ducked, bobbed, weaved; first dashing one way and then back again. Brown curly heads undulated up and down like massive versions of children's hobbyhorses. Curved black horns narrowly passed by. Jerry slipped with his heavy load. Kathy helped to pull him up from one knee. He held on to her attempting to keep from becoming separated. Visions of trampled bodies flashed through his head and made him all the more determined to edge to the side of the herd. Suddenly the mass of woolly monoliths changed direction as if the herd was one ship on a foamy billowing sea.

Snow cascaded off the beasts creating a secondary snowstorm. Their hoofs kicked up more snow. Swirling eddies of white fluff reduced visibility to almost zero. It was a sluggish stampede at first, because the buffalo had been jolted out of sleep. Then it grew in intensity, attaining full speed. Now the ground shook. Jerry tried to defend Kathy from the onrush, but the forms materializing out of the haze were too formidable to oppose. They ended up dodging back and forth and finally running with the shaggy convoy in a worried attempt not to be trampled. Running forward while looking backward, it was only a matter time before they stumbled into substantial sagebrush and mixed legs and arms in a jumble. Jerry could see even less of the oncoming stampede and elected to cover Kathy with his body. The herd galloped by with the buffaloes in the rear, passing them without a single concern. The animals were more accustomed to humans than the reverse. The herd had moved on collective instinct after the initial shock. The pair huddled and shivered in emotional fright, catching their breath and counting the lucky stars hidden above the thick clouds. They lay on the wet trodden ground to collect mutual strength to stand up. Icy cold mud caked hands and faces. They groveled to knees, shaking off frigid slime. To clean off the mess, they used clumps of undisturbed snow as frozen bars of soap. Helping each other, they stood on shaky legs and tried to get their bearings. Jerry lost his sense of direction in the dark. He tried to plan.

"Which way should we go?" he asked Kathy.

"We were going downhill. We might as well keep doing that until we have a better idea."

Jerry nodded in agreement. His hair was soaked. His windbreaker was wet and useless as a barrier to the cold. He was miserable, and when he looked at Kathy, he couldn't figure how she could keep going.

"So, what are you thinking?" Jerry asked.

"I was dreaming about a Caribbean island with white sandy beaches and me basking in the sun, laying at the water's edge, with warm waves tickling my feet."

"Oh, that's not what I was thinking," Jerry answered in surprise.

"What were you thinking?"

"That I'm *freezing* and I won't be able to find my fingers 'cause they dropped off back there where the herd trampled them into the mud!"

"I like my thoughts better," Kathy responded.

"I do too. Can I jump into your dream?"

Kathy had an answer leap to her lips, about the fact that he was already there, but had to stifle it. "Sure, join me. I was just going to order a Mai Tai."

"I'll say one thing for you, you know how to dream."

In silence they walked side-by-side down the field. The snow stopped, and a sleety drizzle took its place. They crossed another fence line and then another. They almost bumped into the building. It was a stable. One side had a large double door with no lock. It had a gabled roof. They looked at each other in disbelief. It wasn't a sandy beach, but it would do. They snuck inside. From the dim light they could see a lantern hanging on a peg by the door. A box of matches sat on a small shelf. They lit the lantern and used its meager heat to warm their hands. Horses inhabited several stalls and snorted their greeting. The body heat from the animals made the stable bearably warm. The stable had six stalls—four along one wall and two on the other. Horses occupied three of them. A large stack of hay bales occupied the corner nearest the door; at the far end of the building was a small area used for tack with pegs holding reins and ropes. A wheelbarrow stood in the middle between the stalls. It was filled with horse manure and had a large scoop shovel with a round wooden handle on the end sitting upside down over the manure. It was a welcome relief to be sheltered. They took off the outerwear and shook the wet from it, then spread the windbreakers on the hay. Their hands went back to the lantern for more heat.

"We can make a bed of straw and it will be warmer than last night. I wish we had some steaks we could grill." Jerry was using Kathy's dream stratagem.

"I think I have a solution to your horrendous appetite." Kathy moved toward the tack section. "Usually horse owners provide oats for their stock."

"And you know this…how?" he questioned.

"I used to work as an ostler for a ranch on the edge of town. I learned a lot about horses and even more about mucking out the stalls." She pointed to the wheelbarrow as she walked by. "It's always been my dream to own horses," she explained. Jerry followed her to the end of the barn. There were two galvanized garbage cans standing next to each other. Kathy popped the lid on one and with her other hand pointed to the contents, her head tilted in the direction of the can. Jerry looked inside.

"You're suggesting we eat horse food."

"Why not? It's just cereal. You do eat cereal, don't you? You're not a complete carnivore." To prove her point, Kathy took a handful and ate some then offered a handful to Jerry. "It's actually good tasting. They roll the oats with a little molasses. Horses love them."

Jerry took a few tenuous bites. He was surprised and popped the whole handful in his mouth. Raging starvation took over, and he grabbed for more. "Yub, You're mrib, This…goob!" Jerry's mouth was crammed full in hungry haste. They ate standing by the saddles and brushes. A strong smell of leather permeated the air.

They ate until they were full and then planned where to sleep. Kathy couldn't resist greeting the horses and feeding them some oats too. Then they made a space to sleep behind the bales and stashed the duffle tote between two bales covered with hay. All evidence of their presence was erased, including the lantern back on its peg. Their gear was with them in the hideout. They had more room than the night before, and they used a couple of saddle blankets over the thermal blanket. It couldn't be warmer, yet Kathy still made a request, "I'm still a little cold from the wet clothes. Can you get a little closer?" Jerry accommodated and could not see her broad smile in the pitch dark.

CHAPTER 4

It was still dark but no longer stormy. Jerry rambled around in the dark to climb over the bales and get to the lantern. It was almost 4 a.m. He lit the lantern and returned to wake Kathy. She was already sitting up. "We need to leave before someone comes to let the horses out to graze." Jerry took the two saddle blankets and started toward the other end of the stables.

"I'll put these back where we found them and get breakfast."

"I'm going to need to use the little ladies stall near the door. I'll join you in a minute." She was pulling hay out of her hair and brushing it off her shirt.

"Don't forget the blueberry yogurt. It'll go great with the oats." Jerry was upbeat.

"You forgot to wash the spoons, remember?" She stumbled over the hay barrier and thought of how good it felt to be warm and not tired.

Jerry was not making a lot of noise scooping out oats and choosing the large clumps that had a tad more molasses, but it was enough to block the creak of the door and the quiet entry of Bradley. He crept down the center aisle. When he had Jerry completely in view he used a line like out of a western movie. "Put your hands up! Don't move or I'll shoot ya!" Jerry dropped oats as he obeyed. "Where's the other one? Ya know, your partner," Bradley demanded.

"She left. She didn't want to stay the night in a stinky barn." Bradley quickly looked around the stable.

"Where's the money?"

"What money?"

"The money you've been carrying on your back—that money. You can't fool me."

"So you want your stolen money back?"

"It's not stolen. It's our money. People gave it to us. It belongs to the Patriot Posse." Bradley straightened his shoulders.

"Why would anyone want to give you, or this Patriot Posse, money?"

"'Cause we're going to be the police someday."

"What?"

"Just gimme the money and shut up."

"I buried it."

"Where? In here?"

"No. On the hill."

"Liar!"

"No, it's the truth. I didn't want to get caught with stolen money or have anyone else find it."

"Tell me where it is."

"I can't."

"You will."

"It's in a difficult place. I would have to show you."

"Tell me. I'll find it."

"No, if I tell you then you'll kill me, and then you'll never find it."

"I'll kill you anyway." Bradley pulled the trigger; the bullet hit the concrete floor and ricocheted into the oat can to the right of Jerry's leg. He jumped. The horses jumped and skittered to the far wall of their stalls, snorting disapproval.

"All right, all right! I'll take you there and show you myself."

Bradley didn't hear the word *myself*, because the lights went out. There was not a ringing sound or star sparkles in his vision.

His vision neither became hazy nor faded to black. One second he was listening, and the next second all cognition ceased. Bradley lay flat on his face while Kathy stood over him with the manure shovel. The shovel was up and ready in case she needed to administer a second blow.

"Took you long enough. I wonder how he found us," Jerry mused as he came forward to take the gun away.

"He probably followed our tracks in the snow," Kathy suggested. Jerry put the gun on safety and checked Bradley for a pulse.

"He's still alive. But I don't think he'll wake up until the next century. We should get going anyway, just in case. Jerry checked Bradley's pockets and found another clip of ammunition and a silencer. He showed Kathy.

"That's pretty fancy weaponry," she said.

"Yeah, it's a Walther PPK—the James Bond gun. He must like the movies. If the wrong guys find us, it might come in handy," Jerry explained.

"And if the right guys find us, namely the police, it will make our story even more unbelievable," Kathy worried out loud.

"We'll just have to make sure we get to the right people without the wrong stuff. But, I'm glad I have this to even the odds. So far we have been bringing shovels to a gun fight." Kathy smiled, and they collected the gear, over-stuffed the pockets of their windbreakers with oats, and turned to go. Abruptly Kathy stepped back to the wheelbarrow and dumped the whole load on Bradley.

"Nice touch," Jerry observed. They blew out the lantern and left.

"Do you believe him?" Kathy asked.

"I think so. Maybe."

"Why would you believe him? He's a thief and a killer. Well, ready to kill to be more precise."

"It sounded like he was bragging instead of lying. When I called it stolen money, he said it belonged to 'us' not 'me.' He used that word. He's responsible for losing their money, and that's why he came looking for us alone. If he doesn't get it back, he'll suffer the same fate as the guy they shot."

"Okay, then if the money is not stolen and belongs to those executioners, then we still don't want to hand it back to them. I doubt they told the police about the missing money. They would want to hide it, right? How could they explain to the police why they have a bag of money and it was in the stolen car?" Kathy tried to clarify.

"This is unbelievable! We're holding unstolen money killers want back, and we're being chased by good guys and bad guys. This is more complicated than a Zane Gray western," Jerry remarked.

"I wonder how much money is in there?"

"I'm not stopping to count it now. I'm getting out of Dodge before the posse shows up."

"All right, I just want you to know that using clichés is a low form of humor," Kathy smirked.

"What do you mean? It *is* a posse that's chasing us, right?" Jerry acted innocent.

"What do you make of this Patriot Posse he spoke of?" Kathy changed to another piece of information they got from Bradley.

"Must be some sort of vigilante group."

"But planning to become the police and killing people at the same time! It doesn't make sense. It's ridiculous!"

"Sometimes these secret societies have a good idea, and then they stray off track. You know, get their purpose mixed up with their importance. I've met some who believe wholeheartedly in a cause and they get lost in the details. Remember Chuck?"

"You mean Corporal Staley? The guy who got chaptered out of the army mid-tour for possession of drugs?"

"Yes."

"Was he one of them?"

"Probably, maybe not this posse group, I don't know for sure, but he couldn't stop talking about his friends back home that owned all these weapons, and they would be the keepers of the peace when the country dissolved into anarchy. He wanted me to join them. He gave us neat little gifts as incentives—knives, compasses, and stuff. After a while I ignored him."

"Interesting...Jerry? Getting to this town, Bailey may not be far enough away from those who are looking for us. Maybe we should try to get to a bigger town or city."

"Like Denver?"

"Yes, I think so."

"If I remember right, the highway through Bailey goes to Denver, but that's another long hike."

"We're making this up as we go along. Maybe we'll think of something when we get there."

The deer trail they were following coincidentally headed north and made their movement easier. It led to a creek, and then they were pushing through brush and pine boughs once again. The walk was tedious. As they lost altitude, the plant life thinned out and gave way to arid ground and dispersed trees. By noon they found themselves staring at a developed road, CO HWY 72, which they avoided walking down. Then they met and used a number of feeder roads. Jerry thought it might be the outskirts of Bailey. He had missed Bailey by two miles to the east. They found Mockingbird Lane and Raven, Lark, and Bluebird Roads. "I guess this is for the birds," Jerry said. They were nervous about being in a residential neighborhood even though the upscale houses were separated by loads of pines and rolling hills. They were startled by a voice.

"Are you guys lost?" a man standing by his rural mailbox asked.

"Ah, sort of. Which way to the highway?

"Straight down until it joins seventy two, and that'll lead ya to the main highway."

"Thank you, sir. We appreciate it."

The couple followed the directions and found five minutes later a station wagon following. They moved to the side of the road. The same man spoke out of his window. "Which way are ya headed?"

"We're trying to get to Denver."

"Well, hop in. We're going there right now."

Kathy looked at Jerry; Jerry looked a Kathy. Jerry touched the jacket pocket where he had the pistol. "Okay, thanks, sir." They could see they would be in the back seat, and they had the security of the revolver.

They made themselves comfortable by pushing the bag and backpacks in the back and leaning against the cushioned seat. It felt so good. Jerry resisted the urge to rub his shoulders that were raw to the touch.

"Hi. I'm Margret, and this is my husband Bert."

"My name is Kathy, and this is Jerry. Nice to meet you." Kathy took the lead in pleasantries.

"Are you married?" Margret inquired.

"No, just out to enjoy nature together."

"It looks like you've been out in it for a while." Bert looked in the rear view mirror.

"Ah, well, we kinda got caught in the snow storm and lost our way," Jerry hastened to clarify. We need to get down to town and stop our friends before they come pick us up tomorrow. We decided to leave early after the storm," Jerry fabricated quickly.

"I'm curious, why did you give us a ride? We're total strangers," Kathy asked.

"Because you said 'sir.' Young people usually don't say 'sir' nowadays. Not unless they have been or are in the military. Are you two in the military?"

"Yes, we are. We just got back from Afghanistan. We thought we would see a little of Colorado before we went home."

"Thank you for your service. I'm retired military myself," Bert commented.

Jerry and Kathy both sensed that this couple was unaware of the manhunt focused on them. They relaxed and talked of their duties in Afghanistan. Bert explained a little of where he had been posted in the army. Margret was more interested in knowing if they were a couple. Kathy helped Jerry by explaining they were just friends. The car made its way down the winding mountain highway and out onto the plains. They entered the built-up areas and then approached Federal Boulevard. Bert indicated that they would have to turn off the highway, which was now called Hampden Ave., to get to their destination to the north.

"Would you mind if we let you off on the corner? You might be able to get more rides at that intersection anyway."

"That would be great. Can we help with your gas? We really appreciate the lift," Jerry offered.

"No, that wouldn't be necessary. We were already coming this way."

"But you saved us a long walk."

"Oh nonsense, people who live up where we live help each other all the time."

Jerry snuck a ten out of his wallet and set it underneath his leg. Kathy caught the movement and smiled. They parted and wished each other well. They found themselves staring at the complex of shops and one small motel.

"I wonder where the nearest police station is," Jerry posed.

"I guess we'll have to look it up. I see a pay phone over there by the motel. Maybe it'll have a phone book. You know, as I think of it, a warm shower is a higher priority for me than the police station. I've been in the same clothes for three days. I don't want to go into the police smelling like sweat and horse leather. Let's get a room and stash our stuff and use the room phone. I really need to call my folks. They must be worried sick. I told them I'd be home two days ago." Kathy wanted some normality to return to her life. They went to the desk and Jerry paid with his debit card. The room represented sanctuary, warmth, and rest. Jerry flopped on the bed. Kathy went to the phone. Her mother answered on the third ring.

"Katie, sweetheart, we've been worried sick. What's going on? The police were here asking questions."

"The police were there?"

"Yes, and they said you and a Gerald Svenson are suspected of stealing a car. Is that true?"

"No, mother, it's not true."

"Then how come you didn't come home like you said, or call us and tell us what's happening?"

"It's a long story. But, we didn't steal a car. Jerry and I are caught in a situation of false circumstances, and we're going to the police station to clear this all up. We should be able to come home after tomorrow."

"Where are you? The police wanted to know your whereabouts. They wanted to know if we knew anything, if you had called home. We're supposed to call them as soon as we hear from you. What should we do, I mean say?"

"Mother, everything is going to be all right. Don't worry. Jerry and I have got the information that will prove we didn't steal a car. The reason I haven't been able to call you is because we've been in the mountains in a snow storm." Kathy didn't want to frighten her mother with any more information than what she already had.

"Who's this Jerry person? Is he a good person? Is he the reason you're in trouble?" Mrs. Pelletier wanted answers.

"Mother, Jerry is a good friend. Remember I told you he helped me when Al broke it off. I trust him, and he's helping me now. Don't worry, Mom, tomorrow it will be like nothing happened. Okay?"

"Okay."

"I'll call again tomorrow, when I get a chance." Kathy wanted to talk more and reassure her mother, but she thought of something serious. She immediately turned to Jerry to find him in exhausted slumber.

"Jerry! Jerry, wake up! We've got a problem. Jerry!" He couldn't see clearly. His eyes ached. All he had to prove he slept was a mouth full of cardboard.

"Ah, um, what's wrong? How long have I been asleep?"

"Jerry, I talked to my mom. She said the police visited them asking if they know where we are. Jerry that means the police know who we are, they know our names!"

"What? They know us? Oh wait, they must have of gotten my name off of the truck...and our army paperwork. Our leave papers are in the folders."

"Do you know what this means?" Kathy sounded like she was a teacher talking to a young student. Jerry rubbed his eyes again and sat up. "Jerry, it means they can track us. You used your debit card to pay for this room. It's only a matter of time before they'll be knocking on this door!"

"You're right. You're right! I should have thought about that. We need to get out of here now!" They needed only to pick up the bags and start for the door. Jerry took the room key and tossed it on the TV. Kathy looked out the window, and Jerry cracked the door. It looked safe so they slipped out and walked as nonchalantly as possible to the end of the building and then hastily down the service alley behind the shops. They were two blocks away up a sharp incline on a side street when they saw from another connecting road a police car rush down Federal Blvd in the direction of the motel. From the higher vantage point on the hill, they were able to see two squad cars race up Hampden Ave and turn on to Federal Blvd from the opposite direction. They dodged between two houses and over the fence. Behind that house was another row of houses for the next block.

They again jumped a chain-link fence and moved toward the back fence. An angry dog attacked at full speed, teeth barred and saliva flying. Jerry moved between the dog and Kathy. His pant leg and part of his leg were locked in vice-like jaws. Kathy took one pack off and swung it with all her might at the head of the cur. A *clunk* resonated because of equipment, including the plastic first aid kit inside the pack. The dog's head was dislodged by the impact.

Free of the dog, Jerry kicked with his foot connecting with its shoulder, propelling the canine several feet away. Jerry slung the moneybag off of his back and used it as a shield as they backed to the fence. Kathy made another swing at the head, which the canine was wise enough to back away from.

Their rear ends bumped into the fence. Jerry let Kathy cross first, and she administered prohibiting swings, allowing Jerry to follow. Without taking a moment to wipe nervous sweat off their brows, they ran up a dead-end road due east into an open field. Police cars started to fan out and cruise up and down nearby streets. The couple doubled back into a wooded yard and found a child's playhouse in which to hide. They huddled there for an hour and then slipped out and down the field. They walked through a drive-in movie theater and up over Santa Fe Drive. They saw a city bus coming and used it to ride southward while they slouched down in the back seats. Jerry examined his torn pants and bleeding leg.

"My gut says we can't talk to the police here either. What do you think?" Jerry asked.

"I think you're right. They must now have our descriptions from the motel clerk. What should we do?"

"We can't just keep going on and on. We've got to end this. And you have to be as tired as I am. We need some sleep. I'm starting to make mistakes in my thinking..." Jerry stopped to concentrate. "Okay, they know we wanted to sleep, and they know we settled for a cheap motel. We change that and we go to a nice hotel, and we pay cash." I have several hundred dollars in my wallet I was planning on using for the trip home. We can get clean and rest and make a move to a police station and get in the door before they arrest us."

"Where are we going to find a nice hotel?"

"Right over there. See the letters on top of the building?" Jerry pointed. It was a virtual feeling of relief to see a place to rest. The five-story building beckoned them. Kathy made a suggestion that she would sign in using cash, and Jerry could come in later with their bags. They mutually decided they needed a balcony room, which would afford them a means of escape should they need it.

At reception she couldn't show her driver's license. She had to improvise. She flopped on the front desk in not-so-mock exhaustion.

"Oh what a horrible day!" she breathed out.

"Can I help you?" the desk clerk asked.

"We, my husband and I, need a room and a hot shower to help forget."

"What's wrong?" the clerked sounded concerned.

"Well, for starters. Our car was stolen with everything in it. Our luggage, our IDs, my husband's wallet, my purse—oh my, my favorite purse! Then the police officer was not the least bit sympathetic. Luckily my husband made a quick ATM withdrawal so we would have something before we called our bank and stuff to cancel everything. Can I get a room key? I'm destroyed by all this stress."

"Yes, ma'am. How do you want to pay for the room?"

"Cash, of course. I'm so glad my husband thought of the ATM or we would have been sleeping under a bridge somewhere," Kathy explained. She placed two hundred in wrinkled twenty-dollar bills on the counter. "This should cover things, and we can settle up tomorrow morning. May I have two room keys please?"

The clerk made the keys and refused a five-dollar tip as an empathetic gesture. Kathy trudged to the elevator and found Jerry loitering nearby but out of sight from the front desk. The room was elegant compared to the stable and five star compared to the juniper bush. Jerry stowed the backpacks in the closet and then placed the bag on the luggage rack.

"I like horse stables, but this is great!" She pulled off her hiking boots and asked if she could be first in the shower. Jerry consented. He wanted the answer to something that nagged at the back of his mind. He took the bag to the table. He started to count the bundles of money and tally them on a hotel notepad.

Kathy came out of the bathroom wrapped in a bath towel with another turban-style on her head. Jerry glanced up from his work and went down to his tally sheet, then he whiplashed his eyes toward Kathy again. Then he dropped his face to the table with a red tinge to his Scandinavian features. Kathy had to smile at his reaction and awkwardness. "Your turn," she remarked.

"Kathy, you've got to see this!"

"What is it?" She came near, and the smell of the shampoo on her hair was intoxicating. He maintained his focus even though the temptation to look pulled with a mighty heave.

"There's a lot more money than I thought. There's over seven hundred thousand in cash."

"Wow!"

"And that's not all. Look at these." Jerry held out a stack of papers.

"What are they?"

"They're Eurobonds. They were at the bottom of the bag. I don't know what they're worth exactly, because these are issued in Germany, and these are issued in Italy. The amounts are in yen and dollars. See, look at these and these. I've been trying to think why would a Eurobond be listed in dollars, or yen for that matter?"

"Maybe Euro dollars?" Kathy queried.

"That's what I first thought, and then I looked at the dates. The Euro dollar didn't start until 1999. The bonds are dated way before that in the early eighties and late seventies. And look they have no names on them. I think anyone can cash them. Like the old Bearer bonds that are now outlawed in the States. Why would someone just hand them over to the posse if they had to be cashed by a particular person or an agent?"

"So what are you telling me?"

"I'm saying that if these are American dollars and the equivalent in yen there must be somewhere around three million dollars here, mostly in these sheets of paper! Free to anyone who has them in their possession."

"Are you sure about the total?"

"Well not for sure. I need to check this out to get the total perfectly accurate. Hey, we need to get some food and stuff at the store. Come on, let's go."

"Jerry, I can't. I washed my underwear in the shower, they're still wet."

"Oh, I see. Well…I saw a Walmart down the street. They have nice greeters at the door. I don't think they'll mind a lady in towels coming to shop."

"You know…that's not a bad idea!" Kathy turned and went toward the door.

"What? You're not thinking I…you…you…you aren't going down there in… What are you doing?"

Kathy snickered at Jerry's reaction as she turned into the bathroom door, which was next to the exit door. Jerry relaxed when she disappeared into the bathroom and closed the door. Two minutes later she came out in her jeans and shirt. The jeans still showed her scraped knee through the damaged hole. She marched toward Jerry.

"I'm going to get some new clothes, and the posse's going to pay for them!" She snatched a wad of bills out of a bundle, checked to see if they were hundreds, and shoved them into her pockets. She looked at Jerry to see if he was coming. He sat surprised. Then he moved.

"Wait a second, I'll go too. You shouldn't be alone. Let me put this away." He shoved the bundles into the bag and took the three thick stacks of bonds and hid them under a mattress. He was about to zip the bag and put it into the closet, but he hesitated. He reached in and extracted several bills for himself too. "The posse owes me a new laptop!" They left.

Outside, as they made their way down the street, Jerry spoke to Kathy, "I thought you couldn't go because your—ah, things are wet."

"They are."

"Wasn't that a problem before? That was why you couldn't go downstairs, right?"

"Right, and I wouldn't. Not unless it was an extreme emergency."

"So why are you... Oh, I get it. You're going Comanche!"

Kathy smiled and said nothing.

They didn't go overboard with a spree. They knew they had to carry what they bought. Jerry got another shirt, some socks, underwear, and a small laptop with extra discs and jump sticks. Kathy found a little more. She added a larger backpack that could carry more than the daypacks they had been using. They snatched some canned chili and Vienna sausages near the checkout. Kathy went straight to the bathroom and exited happier. Jerry was outside the store, putting everything in the pack and calling his folks just in case they had been visited by detectives. He wanted to make sure they were not worried about his delay in coming home. They hoofed it down to the hotel and went to the room.

The first thing Jerry did was get the laptop up and functional with his personal settings and password. His first priority was the transfer of the photos and video from the camera's SD chip to his computer and save them to jump sticks for back-up. Kathy had slipped out of her dirty jeans and gave them a washing in the sink. She tried on the new clothes and then put on a very comfortable long T-shirt that had "Colorado High Country" printed on it with a picture of snow-capped peaks. She sat on the edge of the bed near Jerry.

"Ahem, Jerry, do you think we ought to e-mail the video to the police?"

"Which ones and where? We don't know who might be involved with this posse. And… there's the possibility that whoever got it would dismiss it as a hoax or an attempt at discrediting the police from people on the run."

"How so?" Kathy asked.

"Well, remember those computer jockeys that made that fake video on YouTube? You know the ones that made it look like a large bird swooped down on a tot in the park and carried him away?"

"Yes, I remember that."

"I was thinking that it would be better to hand over the video and have it accompany our sworn statements in person. Do it right from the start before someone can manufacture a response about it being a fake or contrived by us," he said.

"I see, and being there in person lets the police see our sincerity."

Jerry rubbed his eyes, and Kathy had a faraway look. "I'm going to get a shower. I'm tired," he said. Kathy picked up one of the Eurobonds Jerry had on the table and examined it. It didn't look all that impressive. She pulled back the cover to one of the double beds and laid on one side deep in thought. She was still thinking when Jerry came and turned out the lights, double checked the night locks on the door, and slipped into the other bed. The revolver was on the nightstand between them.

"Jerry?"

"You're still awake?"

"Yes. I've been thinking about the money. The posse should not get their money back. They may have gotten it legally, gifts and stuff, but I can't see turning the money over to people who kill people. We would be supporting their criminal behavior."

"I had the same thought, but I don't know what to do with it…ah, properly. It's tempting to keep it. I, like you, think they owe us for what they put us through. They should at least pay us for what we lost."

"That's another problem. I don't think they'd be willing to reimburse us if we asked."

"You've got that right. We'll stash the money, get this cleared up with the police, and figure out what we're going to do with it after that. Unless you have another plan?"

"The problem is getting there and which 'there' is going to listen to us fairly." Thinking about those problems made the room quiet, and two ticks later they were both asleep.

CHAPTER 5

Anight clerk slipped the bill under the door just after 6 a.m. Both heard the minimal sound, but Jerry reacted in a flash, grabbing the gun, sitting up, and pointing it at the door. Early-morning light lent shadows in corners a different appearance. He drew quick beads on each in turn and then back to the door. He relaxed, seeing the envelope illuminated by the hall light under the door space.

"A little jumpy this morning?" Kathy asked.

"I guess. I had a dream where I was cornered, and a mountain lion wanted the dead rabbit I had in my hand. But it was downtown in an alley with trash cans filled with oats."

"That'd be a no brainer for a dream analyst to figure out. I woke up several times thinking somebody was in the room."

"Did you dream at all?" Jerry asked as he put the gun back on the night table.

"Yes, I dreamt I was home and Mom was in the kitchen making pancakes."

"You dream better than me."

They lay in the beds and stared at each other. After coming to the conclusion that sleep was not to return, Jerry remarked, "Well, another day of playing dodge 'em."

"What are we going to do?"

"Eat!" Jerry slipped out of his bed on the opposite side from Kathy and immediately jumped into his jeans. Kathy watched.

His back was well defined with muscles. She caught a glimpse of his shorts before the jeans were all the way up. When he turned on the lights, she could see his bare chest. He had an even better defined six-pack of abs and pecks. The light illuminated the soft gold layer of body hair against bronze skin. She was thinking about how she had the impression that only his face and arms had been tanned from the Afghan sun. Now she knew his Adonis look was complete from body to brain. She was so into her thoughts she didn't think when she tossed back the covers to get up. The long nightshirt had ridden up over her hips almost to her rib cage. Seeing her caught Jerry by complete surprise. There was a momentary gawk by Jerry before Kathy hastily pulled the hem down. She didn't miss, however, his attraction. For a moment she was ashamed that it had happened and then she was kind of pleased with herself.

"I've got an idea. Instead of going out to find breakfast or eating some more of those linkettes, let's call room service. We can stay inside out of view until we're ready," Kathy suggested.

Jerry was standing at the door looking at the bill. "It shows we still have a positive balance. Let's get a big breakfast."

"One like the army?"

"Yeah."

"I'll phone it in."

"I drank too much water last night." Jerry ducked into the bathroom. When he came out later, Kathy was dressed and organizing their stuff.

"We still need to decide what we're going to do," Kathy stated.

"Maybe we should try a police department on the other side of Denver from the mountains. Do you think they might be less involved in our case?"

"Could be. Or we could try the police in Colorado Springs close to Fort Carson. They might be a little more sympathetic to returning soldiers. But that would represent another long walk."

"We could ride a bus, maybe."

"Yeah, FREX."

"What's FREX?"

"It's an acronym. It means Front Range Express. It goes between Denver and Colorado Springs." We can ask the front desk where the nearest stop might be. If we can get a place where the bus stops for passengers, then it will take us to downtown Colorado Springs." Jerry was already planning their next move. He needed to get to a south-side stop. He reacted to a knock at the door and immediately relaxed when he heard, "Room service."

Kathy answered the door. "Breakfast for Mr. and Mrs. Arbuckle." The porter pushed the cart in the door and stationed it near the small table. Kathy handed him a tip because Jerry was momentarily frozen. As the porter retreated out the door, he came out of his trance,

"Ah, sir?"

"Yes."

"Does the hotel shuttle go to the airport?"

"Yes, of course."

"Does it make stops along the way, or does it go direct?"

"It stops at our sister hotels in Greenwood Village and another at the airport."

"Greenwood Village…is that the place where the FREX stops?"

"Yes, near there, why?"

"Oh, nothing really, just trying to remember something near there, thank you."

The porter closed the door when he left. Jerry looked at Kathy and said, "Mr. and Mrs. Arbuckle, huh?" Kathy blushed.

"They used the name I gave at the front desk," Kathy answered. Jerry picked up the invoice lying on the bed and read the "billed to:" line. It read the same as the porter's address. "Okay, I guess that's better than the alternative and calling attention to ourselves. Let's eat!"

They pulled off lids and found what Kathy had ordered. It looked like a feast for four people—double plates of eggs, bacon, and hash browns, with juice. Jerry pointed at the blueberry yogurt.

"Do you have any leftover oats?"

"Do you like it?"

"Yes. Blueberry yogurt is my favorite. I see you ordered pancakes."

"The power of nocturnal suggestion," Kathy quipped.

"So, you transform your dreams into reality. Can you dream a nice conclusion to this mess we're in?"

"Already have."

They began breakfast quietly, and then Kathy turned on the TV. She searched for a local news channel and found one that they remembered served both Denver and Colorado Springs. They watched and ate. It felt good to dine sedately rather than gulp and gallop as they were used to. Cloth napkins were a luxury they did not experience in the last year. When finished, Jerry put a phone book on the table and searched Greenwood Village from the maps in the front section. He found the sister hotel and the FREX stop both marked on the map.

"Well, all we have to do is catch the shuttle there and wait out of video range until a bus comes."

"It looks like a plan." They pulled on the pack and the black bag. Jerry tucked the PPK into his belt under the windbreaker. They turned to leave and heard the reporter beginning a story about returning soldiers from Afghanistan. They stopped to listen.

"*Two soldiers are on a rampage, possibly suffering from recent battle shock. The police indicated gunshots fired and stolen cars. The manhunt has been over mountains and rugged terrain. What we have been able to learn of this unfolding story comes from different sources.*"

The picture changed to a police officer being interviewed. The caption under the video read, "Lieutenant Webber."

"*We saw the two fugitive car thieves driving a car that matched the description of a stolen vehicle. Police set up a roadblock, and when*" *these two saw the roadblock, they fled over the mountains. Units are out searching for them now."*

The picture changed to another view with another plainly clothed officer talking. "Detective Soriano" of the CSPD was written under his image.

"As a rule we don't comment when it comes to ongoing investigations. However, I would like to advise these two soldiers to come into the office and tell their story. There are some ambiguities that need to be explained."

The video came back to the studio, and the reporter said, "We have learned that the two suspects have recently returned from a tour of duty in Afghanistan. Their names are Sgt. Gerald Svenson and Sgt. Katherine Pelletier. They were recently interviewed upon their return."

Kathy's picture filled the screen.

The interviewing reporter was off screen but could be heard asking, *"What's it like being in war as a woman? Were you nervous? Afraid?"*

"Well, after I was there for a couple of months, it seemed like normal, maybe a little boring." The picture started with her talking and then changed to a view of her uniform.

"Did you see a lot of violent action?" The picture came back on her face, and the microphone covered her mouth. Her words were clipped.

"I was in a convoy that came upon a roadside bomb. One died. He was a friend. I felt anger."

Next Jerry's face appeared. And his interview abruptly began. His expression looked almost worried to almost angry.

"Now that you're home, what are your plans?"

"My plans? My plan…I guess I'll execute my plan as soon as I get my chance."

"There you have it here on Channel Eight News. If you have any information on the whereabouts of these two individuals, please contact police."

Jerry and Kathy sat on the bed, side by side, staring at the television set. It took them a little time to collect their thoughts.

"Well, now we know the name of the boss who ordered the killing—Lieutenant Webber. He's a police officer! That explains a lot!" Jerry erupted.

"They clipped my words! They made it sound like I was an angry woman!" Kathy spouted. They both shook their heads in disgust. "People are going to be able to identify us easier."

"And that Officer Webber is a dirt ball. We can't have him around if we're going to get this reported." Jerry maintained his focus on the enemy.

"Jerry, that Detective Soriano seems fair. He didn't class us as car thieves. We might be able to trust him, maybe."

"That gives us a possible place to start. I have an idea. When we get down to the Springs, we'll call him and set up a meeting, then we'll watch the place to see if a bunch of patrol cars show up. Then we'll know. If he comes alone just to talk, we give it a try. If not, and I just thought of this, we'll make the meeting place be close to the station and while they're watching for us there, we'll slip into the station without a lot of policemen in the way," Jerry postulated.

"Good thinking. Before we go though, I'm going to buy a wig and a different-colored jacket. It would be good if you changed your look a little too. There's a gift shop on the main floor. I don't think we have to settle up at the front desk. We're not over the amount I gave them last night, and the room service charge won't put us over the top. I'll just put the key on the desk and say everything's fine. I'll do it when they're busy." Jerry listened to Kathy verbalizing her plan. He liked the way she put things together.

The shuttle left on the hour, so they had to wait forty minutes. They hid out in the bar after shopping in the store. The gift shop didn't have wigs, so Kathy got a floppy sun hat. Jerry got a ball cap. They both bought sunglasses and fleece pullovers of different colors so as not to call too much attention as a couple with "Mile High City" and a small skyline imprinted on the upper left chest. They looked like tourists. The ride took fifteen minutes to Greenwood Village. Jerry didn't need to remember the map because a directional sign to Fiddler's Green and the FREX bus stop guided their steps. They waited in a secluded corner of the lot until the bus arrived, and they sauntered on. They got seats in the back. Their plan was to get off at the south side stop in the city under Interstate 25, between Nevada and Tejon Streets. It would be less than a mile north to the center of town and the most probable place for the police headquarters.

Their breathing increased as they exited the bus. Their nerves were a jangle; they were extremely vigilant and watched cars from every direction. They also spied out good vantage points and meeting places. They found a Starbucks across the street from a two-story restaurant with an upper terrace and a back entrance to an old alley. It was ideal for their purpose. Now they had to stow their bags in a safe place. Three blocks over was a storage facility, Stor-n-lock, with the smallest unit being twenty times larger than they needed. Kathy went in to rent a unit. Jerry waited down the street, behind some stores, with the bags. Kathy returned.

"Done. I got a small one with outside access and they were also selling combination locks, so I bought one as well. The minimum rental was for three months. I don't think the posse will mind the extra cost," Kathy snickered. They walked around the block on the back side to avoid moving past the windows of the office. They dropped the bag and the backpacks inside, and Jerry scanned in every direction before slipping the gun into the moneybag. All they kept was one flash drive with the pictures on it to give to the detective; everything else went to the cavernous storage container. They retraced their path to the restaurant and got a seat in the open balcony overlooking the street and the intersection.

"I think I'll make the call from Starbucks. They probably have caller ID and my request will seem more believable."

"And I'll order us some drinks and appetizers," Kathy added.

Jerry had to take in three deep breaths to calm himself before he made the call. He asked for Detective Soriano. And they had to transfer him through.

"This is Detective Soriano. Who's calling?"

"Hello, sir. I am Gerald Svenson. I heard you wanted to talk to us and clear this mess up."

"Are you Sgt. Svenson?"

"Yes, sir. Sir, could you come down to Starbucks on South Nevada? We can meet you there."

"I think I could do that. But, don't you want to come to the station instead?"

"For now, Starbucks will do."

"Okay, it should take me about ten minutes to get there."

"We'll wait for you. Good-bye." Jerry hung up, checked his watch, and casually left the building. He walked down the street, crossed over, and came up behind the restaurant. He entered by the back parking lot door. He sat down next to Kathy and they watched. Activity remained normal. No police cars or extra cars arrived. Time ticked by.

"It looks like he might trust us. I hope so," Jerry spoke to Kathy looking at the road.

"I think we should begin first with the stolen car. That's the primary focus of the police. If we start from the beginning then he will be wondering about the car, and we might be giving him too much to chew on before we resolve the car issue in his head," Kathy strategized.

"Okay, then we'll calm *his* concerns first and then get to our big concerns second. Good thinking."

Eleven minutes after Jerry ended the phone conversation, a sedan with a small stubby antenna parked in front of the bookstore next to the coffee shop. Detective Soriano was easily recognizable. They watched him walk in without looking around in a suspicious manner. They waited another five minutes. Still no other patrol cars came to surround the store. They decided to make the move across the street. Again the heavy nervous breathing took charge of their bodies. They entered and found the detective sitting at a table with four chairs. Three lattes sat on the table. He arose and spoke kindly.

"Thanks for seeing me. I assume you saw me on TV, and that's why you called me."

"Yes, we did. We thought you would give us a fair hearing."

"That's why I came. Help yourselves to the lattes. Before we begin, let me tell you what I know. I talked with both your parents by phone. I checked with the police records in your state. I called Fort Carson and talked with your unit commander. Everyone tells me you are model citizens, are good soldiers, and have no police records. The only thing I could find on the record was a parking ticket for you, Miss Pelletier. I'm telling you this to set you at ease. I will listen to you with an open mind."

"That's all we ask, sir," Jerry answered.

"Oh, and a couple named Mr. and Mrs. Ferguson, who gave you a lift into Denver, called me and talked to me about you. They don't believe the story about you being criminals. They said you were very respectful and called them 'sir.' And, another thing, they said you left them ten dollars for gas even though they said it wasn't necessary."

"We didn't steal the car," Kathy blurted out.

"Okay, I'll have to be honest with you. Your prints are on the car. Can you explain why?"

Kathy didn't hesitate. "We were forced to steal a car by a guy with a gun, because he wanted Jerry's pickup. He shot at us, I mean toward us, on the ground, and we had no choice but to give him the keys to the truck and get in the car and drive away." The detective started writing notes in a small book. "Then he chased us with the truck and wrecked the truck." Kathy was warming to the topic.

"Why would he chase you if he made you two take the car?"

"We'll have to get to that in a second, but the short answer would be because we were accidental witnesses. We'll explain later," Jerry interjected.

"Okay, then I need to have your reason for running off into the woods instead of coming down the hill to the police road block. Did you see the road block?" Soriano got to his significant question.

"We talked about that when we were fleeing. We said that if we got stopped by the police before we could get to the station to report the crime, the police would be less than inclined to believe our story. Then Jerry saw the police car with its lights on coming to the entrance to the road. We had to do something. Besides, they were firing at us."

"They were shooting at you?"

"Yes, the same guy who wrecked Jerry's truck."

"Okay, I can see you were under duress and made some hasty decisions. If I were you, though, I would have fled to the policeman for protection."

"Maybe you're right from that perspective, but because of what happened, we were glad we fled," Jerry explained. He looked and spoke to Kathy, "I think we need to tell him now about the rest." Kathy agreed with her head. "Sir, because of what we witnessed, we were in danger for our lives." The detective kept writing and spoke as he wrote.

"Yes, he was firing at you. That would scare me too."

"Sir, I'm going to tell you everything starting from the beginning..." Jerry began by describing why they had come to the mountain, giving details of the mountain lion they wanted to film. Then he told him about the group of men digging. He inserted the fact that Lieutenant Webber was the leader. This got a look from Officer Soriano and then he went on writing his notes. Then Jerry described the execution. Detective Soriano stopped. His eyes focused on Jerry with penetrating intensity. His all-business detective face was gone in an instant.

"You saw Lieutenant Webber *shoot* the man in the hole?"

"Yes, sir. Along with the other two Jerry mentioned. That's why we were running for our lives," Kathy added.

"Are you sure this happened? This isn't some kind of battle fatigue flashback, like PTSD?"

"No, sir. We have it on video." Jerry placed the jump stick on the table. Detective Soriano had to collect himself. This case had gone forward because of the eyewitness account of Lieutenant Webber and the gunplay he had reported, which only made it more disconcerting. At this moment he saw a much larger crime with deep ramifications. A senior member of the department was implicated. This would turn everything upside down. If he was wrong, his career would be ruined. If these kids were telling the truth, the department would suffer the scandal for years to come. He had to be careful.

"Ah, Jerry and Kathy, this is a significant accusation and basically answers a lot of my questions about why you acted as you did. However, this needs to be handled properly. I'll need to take that jump drive as evidence, and we need to get you down to the station and make a complete report. I'll make sure your information is handled properly." The detective had an evidence zip-lock bag in his jacket and took it out and opened it. In red letters the bag had the word "EVIDENCE" printed across one side. He opened it for Jerry to drop in the drive.

"Come on, I'll give you a ride." They rose and went out the door.

The tape recorder stayed on for forty-five minutes, recording their story verbatim. They did not include information about the money or the gun they took from Bradley. They explained their fear that they didn't know which police officers were involved in the Patriot Posse. Officer Soriano stayed with them in the inter-rogation room along with another detective, Det. Probasco, and a stenographer who typed out the report to be signed later. At one point, Soriano gave the second detective the evidence bag and asked if the jump drive could be downloaded at the lab and evaluated ASAP. At the end of the session, they waited for a final written report to be finished. Detective Soriano talked about Jerry's pickup. He said it had been brought down for evidence and all of their stuff had been collected off the hillside and brought to evidence storage. He called on his cell and had their personal effects released for them to retrieve. Detective Probasco helped by volunteering to give them a ride, as it was the end of his shift and he was going to the gym. The report came in five copies. They had to read and initial every page and sign all five cop-ies. Detectives Soriano and Probasco signed as witnesses. They were admonished not to leave town and were told they would take rooms at a nearby hotel under police custody, for their safety. They agreed, shook hands, and left with Detective Probasco, who would take them to the evidence storage facility next to the car lot and then return them to the hotel.

Titanic relief permeated their souls. They almost collapsed in the sedan. They wanted to sleep. Their nerves had burnt all their reserves. They no longer had to maintain vigilance for who might be following them. They rode in silence. Detective Probasco wanted to talk, and because they were happy to be over the hump, they showed courtesy in deference to his position.

"Feel better now?"

"Yes, sir, it feels good to have it off of our shoulders and in the hands of the police," Jerry agreed.

"You actually saw the murder? The mind doesn't dismiss that kind of thing easily."

"Yes, it was awful. I never want to see that again," Kathy said, while letting out a lungful of air.

"Your testimony had a lot of information. It will be very significant if this comes to trial. So the Patriot Posse was responsible for the killing?"

"Yes, they were. Do you know anything about this group?" Jerry asked.

"Well, knowledge of the posse surfaced a few years ago, and it never seemed to be a problem. We know they are in every state of the union and are growing bigger. Some very fine community leaders are a part of the organization."

"Does that mean that this group we tangled with is an offshoot or a radical faction that functions separately from the whole?"

"Maybe. Are you sure of your identification of the shooters?"

"We saw Lieutenant Webber do it and might be able to identify the other two if we saw them."

"I can see why Detective Soriano wants to keep you around for verification. Ah, I hope you don't mind a slight delay. I'm going by my house to pick up something I forgot to bring with me this morning. I need it at the gym where I work out. Do you mind? It'll only take a minute."

"Sure, no problem, sir," Jerry agreed. A few minutes later the detective swung his car onto a country road and then abruptly turned into a long driveway to a ranch house. The double garage door opened by remote and Officer Probasco drove in and closed the door behind him. He pulled his revolver and pointed at the couple in the back seat.

"The Patriot Posse is bigger than you think. You've gotten in over your heads. Now where's the money?"

Kathy almost fainted. Jerry fought off panic. They melted into the seat like chocolate in a frying pan. Weak and wasted they could hardly resist when their assailant demanded for them to get out. He repeated his question, "Where's the money?"

"We don't have it," Jerry spoke to the floor.

"I'll give you a choice. Take me to the money now or I'll take you to Commander Webber and we'll beat the crap out of your lover girlfriend."

"We're not lovers," Kathy retorted.

"Don't give me that crap. You're trying to make me believe you don't have any affection for each other. She doesn't look like she can take a lot of beating. We'll get the location out of her, or you, sooner or later."

"You style yourselves as the police of the future! You're nothing but animals!" Kathy had venom in her mouth.

"Things will change soon enough, and society will need us. You two are standing in our way. Turn around. Put your hands against the wall, above your heads."

They did as they were ordered. Officer Probasco smacked Jerry on the side of his head with the butt-end of the revolver. He almost went down. Kathy lurched in his direction, teeth clinched in a silent snarl; she stopped with the muzzle of the gun in her face.

The detective leered. "See I knew you two were lovers. Get back with your hands on the wall." The detective grabbed Jerry's arms and pulled them behind his back. He quickly had his hands in a plastic zip cuff. With Jerry subdued, he approached an angry Kathy. "Hands down behind your back!" She reluctantly obeyed and was cuffed with the same plastic strip as was on Jerry. "Now turn around. Once more, where's the money?"

Jerry had had time to think, and he wanted to buy as much time as possible. "All right, I'll tell you. We buried the money up on the mountain."

"The mountain where you ditched the car?"

"No, near to where we spent the night in the stable. Where we beaned the guy who was following us."

The officer was in thought. "Okay. Let's go."

Probasco opened the trunk to the sedan and demanded, "Get in!" The two were confused until he shoved them toward the trunk. "Get in!" He shoved them with the point of his gun. Jerry did the best he could to assist Kathy to climb in, using his elbow to steady her. Then he got in and lay down. The trunk lid closed with a thud. They heard the garage door motor, and the car started. The wheels scrunched on the gravel at the end of the driveway.

"Kathy?" She didn't answer for a moment.

"Yes, Jerry." Her voice sounded wavy.

"Are you crying?"

"Yes."

Jerry hesitated. "Don't cry. I'm going to get us out of here."

"Okay." Kathy sniffed. He groped with his fingers to find hers. They touched; comfort came through the tips as a soothing balm.

"I need your help." It was what she needed, a straw to grasp.

"What can I do?"

"I'm going to get my wallet out of my pants, and I'm not sure how I'm going to hold it at the same time as I get something out."

"What are you trying to get?"

"I need something inside it. Back me up with your hands?"

"Yes." She adjusted herself to where she could cup his hands. Touching him gave her even more assurance, as slight as it was.

"Okay I'm going to work it out of my pocket." With his hands tightly bound together, with one arm pinned to the bottom of the trunk, and the car bouncing over the road, all this made it more difficult. He knew getting the wallet out was only one slight problem. Holding it open and sliding a credit card out might be more difficult. The wallet came out easily. Getting his fingers to open it was a bit more of a challenge. He dropped it.

"Jerry, what are you after? You're not planning to bribe him, are you?" Her voice was steadier.

"I have a credit card knife."

"You have a knife in your wallet?"

"Yes, it's a special credit card knife."

"During all this you've had a knife and you didn't use it?"

"We never had a need. Remember, you don't bring a knife to a gun fight, especially a knife made of plastic and only about two and a half inches long."

"I've never heard of a credit card knife."

"It's very sharp and has a thin metal edge. I think it can cut through this plastic."

"Okay, let's do it!" Kathy had more spirit. They fumbled the wallet up from the floor. Jerry was able to hold it open and asked Kathy to feel through the cards. "What am I looking for?"

"The card feels different that other cards, slightly thicker. On one edge there are several nubs used to fold and snap the knife into place. Feel for the nubs."

"Are we going to have to assemble it?"

"No, it's all one piece. We just have to flip and fold."

"Okay, I think I've got it. Yes, it feels bumpy." Jerry dropped the wallet and focused on the card.

"Hand it to me. Good." Jerry went silent as he felt for familiar spots on the card. He located the small circle that, when turned, released the blade. He had to turn and try several times to get the exact setting that would clear the blade. When successful he flipped the blade outward and folded the edges in over it to make a handle to hold the blade in place. He squeezed the folded edges and snapped them over the nubs. "I've got it. Now guide my hands to your cuffs. Watch out for the blade point and the edge—they're very sharp. Kathy tenuously felt for his hands and the knife. She centered the knife upon the thick strap.

"Commander, I have them. Yes, I've got them bound in the trunk of my car."

"Good, how did you manage that?"

"I offered to give them a ride from the station to their personal effects and then to the hotel. Then I forced them to tell me where the money is by holding a weapon on them."

"Did they tell you?"

"Sorta. At first they wouldn't, but then I threatened to beat the girl, and the fella gave in. He says they buried the money up near the stable. Bradley can show us where that's at, and we can force their hand there."

"Okay, I'll get Bradley rounded up..."

"Commander, we've got another problem. They signed statements at the station saying they saw you kill the mole. And they had pictures to prove it."

Officer Webber swore. Probasco hastened to help calm his leader. "Soriano asked me to take the jump stick down to the lab and have copies made."

"Did you?" Webber's voice was as deadly as shrapnel.

"I did, but not before I erased it," Probasco proudly added.

Webber was only slightly appeased. "I suppose that bleeding heart Soriano believed their story."

"Pretty much."

"Okay, I'll figure something out. First, bring them to the meeting house, and we'll get the money, and then we'll make them disappear."

"Right, Commander, I'll be there in about forty-five minutes."

Jerry awkwardly sawed at the strap. They had little room to shift, and he needed to be careful not to poke Kathy with the point end. Just when it felt like it wouldn't work, the cuff snapped and fell to the floor. Kathy rubbed her hands and then rolled over in place to take the knife from Jerry. She caressed his hand, feeling for the blade. When she had it, she started on Jerry's cuff. She had better movement and pressure. His cuff came off in half the time.

"Now what are we going to do?" Kathy asked.

"I think we need some light. I need to move around." In the tight space he struggled to position his body along the passenger's side with his feet searching for the right side taillight. Kathy tried to adjust to his movements, and he fumbled over and around her body. The new angle of his torso and legs eliminated her ability to straighten out. She curled into a fetal position.

"What are you going to do?"

"I'm going to kick out the taillight. What I need you to do is make some noise. He knows we're back here so do some complaining and then scream. I'll kick when you scream."

Kathy wasn't entirely play-acting, "Let us out of here!" She pounded on the back of the trunk. "Let us out now! Eeeyyaeeeahh!"

Jerry collided with the housing for the lights and shot it out of the hole in one angry strike from his foot. Light bathed the interior. And the taillight housing dangled by wires and bumped in the wind against the fender. He could see her face and the dried track of tears on her cheeks.

"Next on the agenda is getting out of here," Jerry said. He shifted to see the cover for the spare tire. It had a twist nut with a handle. He pulled up the cover and shoved it to the back of the trunk. He undid the tire iron jack handle and started to pry around the edges of the trunk lid. That's when Kathy saw the little red tab hanging by a wire. In the dim light it read 'pull.' It was a safety feature built into the late model sedan. She pointed it out to Jerry with a slight grin. He stopped his prying.

"Leave it to you to find the easy way out," Jerry said. "Okay, we have to pick our moment of escape." He turned around and looked out the hole. "I'd say we're traveling about fifty, maybe sixty miles per hour. We have to wait until he slows down."

"Or stops. I like stops better," Kathy corrected.

"Okay, tenderfoot, we'll wait for him to stop at a light or a stop sign. Then we'll jump out and run like hell!" he directed.

"But, he'll see us when the trunk pops up. He'll shoot at us."

"Yep. We'll try to get to cover. But, I don't think he'll want to shoot if they're people around. Also, he still needs us to guide him to the money. If he shoots, keep running." They readied themselves for a fast exit. Jerry put his wallet back in his pants, and he stretched out his hands to hold hers. "Don't worry. I'll be right behind you."

Detective Soriano returned from the deli with a pastrami sandwich in a bag and a drink. It only took a few minutes to run across the street. He was worried. The case was ten times bigger than before. He analyzed the information whirling around in his head. He believed them. That was not his problem. He was worried about the bigger problem of criminal activity in his precinct. He had never heard of the Patriot Posse before. The division kept track of organizations of that nature.

How big is this going to get? He asked himself. He ate his sandwich and drank his soda while he scanned the statement once again. The pictures will seal the whole report. He picked up the phone and called the forensics lab.

"Preston, I sent Detective Probasco down there with a jump drive. I asked for the pictures to be downloaded. Do you have them yet?"

"Yes, I have the drive stick, and I'm working on it now. There doesn't seem to be anything on it. I'm checking now to see if there *was* anything on it. What's this all about?"

"It's about a murder. Are you sure there's nothing on it?"

"I'm sure." Detective Soriano hung up the phone and called Probasco immediately.

"Yes, boss. What's up?"

"Where are you? Do you still have them with you?"

"No, boss. They said they were hungry and wanted to get a good meal. I dropped them off at an Olive Garden on Academy Blvd. I didn't think it would be a problem since they said they would find their way back to the hotel when they were done. They wanted to get their stuff tomorrow. I gave them the registration and room numbers. Nice couple. Very respectful."

"Get back to the restaurant and pick them up now. I need to see them ASAP!"

"Boss, that might take some time. I'm already over on the other side of town headed north to my favorite gym. You, or a squad car might get there faster."

"Probasco?" Soriano almost yelled.

"Yes?"

"You're an idiot! You should have stayed with them all the way back to the hotel!" Detective Soriano punctuated his anger by hanging up.

Watching out the back of the sedan, Jerry could see countryside replacing residential space. The road was now two lanes with slow curves. Trees and brush became more prevalent. Red sandstone rocks dotted the landscape. Their nerve endings began to tingle when the car slowed and took a turn. The road bent around to the left and came to a stop sign. Jerry nodded at Kathy, and he pulled the tab. The trunk popped open, and Kathy was out of the trunk in a flash. Jerry was close behind, carrying the tire iron. Probasco was caught completely off guard, frantically struggling with his seat belt. Kathy sprinted to the bushes, and Jerry ran, looking back at the detective.

Probasco ran after them, leaving his car idling on the street. He fired a warning shot to get them to stop. They didn't slow down. Instead they ran faster. He fired with a determination to hit something. Kathy headed for a sandstone formation when the next bullet came at her. Probasco aimed at her because he knew Jerry would stop to aid her. The second bullet was perfectly aimed at her moving form, only the rock intercepted the bullet. Jerry hit the ground as he was trained to do and then crawled to the rocks and began running again.

Probasco was in a delirium of anger. He ran madly at them, making good time. Kathy knew he was following their path, and so she didn't blast out the other side of the rocks but changed her course to keep the rocks between them. She headed for another formation and found a fence blocking the path. She dropped on her side and rolled under the bottom strand. Jerry matched her technique. When the detective rounded the first formation, he saw nothing. He was momentarily confused and swiveled his head in every possible direction. Kathy sprinted away like an Olympian out of the blocks. Jerry scrambled up too. Probasco was able to get another shaky shot away as he sprinted across the uneven ground. It was uphill to the rocks, and they had to climb behind scrub oak bushes. Probasco fired again while running. Kathy edged around behind the formation on a small ledge as Probasco was negotiating the fence. Jerry leaped up the formation in bounding steps that looked to be equivalent to antelope springs. He rounded the rocks and found Kathy had stumbled and rolled into a large crack. She was struggling to get out. Jerry pulled her up and stepped back along the back edge of the rocks and waited. There were no new rock formations close at hand, just a long open slope. Probasco came around the rocks at jet speed. Jerry laid the tire iron across his forehead in an equally fast opposite direction. Probasco was down with all circuits nonfunctioning.

"That looked like an in-the-park homerun," Kathy quipped.

"I learned from the best," Jerry retorted.

"Get his gun. We need it!" Kathy said out of breath. "We're starting with less than we had before." Jerry dropped the tire iron and picked up the revolver.

Detective Soriano drove with lights blinking to Olive Garden. He had called ahead for assistance, meeting the officer at the door. He reported, "Nobody here matches the description you gave." Soriano went inside anyway to check for himself. He walked through every section, checked both male and female bathrooms, and interviewed the receptionists. He started to challenge his previously held opinion about the young soldiers. Innocent victims don't hide and lead people to believe that they have undeniable evidence that did not exist. What didn't jive was their willingness to come in and give such a detailed report. They either had to be prevaricating sociopaths or locked into something behind the scenes. If their disappearance was linked to Officer Webber's foul play, then why would they say they wanted to eat in a public restaurant? He called Detective Probasco's cell phone. He didn't answer. He returned to his office to see if there were any clues in the statement or contradictions from his written notes.

They were in the Garden of the Gods. Picturesque rock formations of pink sandstone jutted upward into giant natural monoliths aimed toward the sky. People say that they look like fingers pointing to the heavens. It is a public park open to all free of charge. The cost for Jerry and Kathy was pumping adrenaline and a dismal outlook on life in general.

"What should we do now?" Kathy asked.

"Let's get to a phone and call Detective Soriano." Jerry hoped that would be the quick solution.

They marched through brush and wind-molded formations. They found a road and walked near it until they saw a sign to the souvenir shop and café. There they had the prospect of a public phone. It was less than a mile.

"I can't believe we're going through this again," Kathy groused.

"We need to get under his safe custody with people he and we can trust," Jerry countered.

"He trusted this Probasco character. I don't think he even knows how prevalent the posse is," Kathy reminded.

"He's got a problem."

"We have a problem," she corrected.

Probasco's phone rang and rang. He was coming out of it with an extreme headache and blurred vision. He fumbled for the device on his belt. "Yesh," he slurred.

"Where are you?"

"…Garden of…Gods."

"You should have been here by now. What's happening?" Commander Webber wanted to know.

"Got away...I mean they got...ooo...ow, my head hurts," he moaned.

Webber could surmise what had happened. "Where are you?"

"Almost...entrance, a little...you know...road." Probasco had a severe concussion; every thought hurt.

Webber gathered the few men he had available, including Bradley, and raced down to the south entrance to the garden. He knew the route Probasco would normally take. He found his car running in the middle of the road, the driver door open and the trunk lid up. The rear brake lights were dangling by the attached wires. He could see the elements of the escape. A man in a beat-up utility van had stopped to investigate. Webber parked and approached. He held up his badge. "The police will take care of this from here, thank you." The man left.

The small contingent looked around for signs and found strong indications in the gravel and dirt leading into the park. They found a shell casing and continued. Probasco had fallen back again on his back. They found him with a large swelling disfiguring his face. Commander Webber directed his men to follow the trail in an open formation and track down the couple. They had their guns, but concealed them out of sight.

"Bradley, you're a good tracker. Find them!"

"Yes, sir!" Bradley's hand came up to his bandaged head and to an off-centered white cowboy hat in half salute. Casualties were starting to mount. He saw the tire iron lying a little behind Probasco. He used a handkerchief to pick it up and shove it into his belt. The tire iron with fingerprints may come in handy. Webber assisted Probasco back down to his own car and sat him in the front seat. He then drove Probasco's car to a hill, got out, and sent the sedan down and off the road into a tree. He returned to his car and drove Probasco to the wreck and helped him into the driver's seat. He called 911.

❈❈❈

On one end of the long porch was the public phone. The curios shop had a southwestern décor with shiny log poles supporting the roof over the porch. Kathy made the call, and Jerry kept vigil. It had taken them awhile to walk around the store and watch cars coming and going. They were worried that the posse could be hiding behind every juniper tree. When they called the first time, Detective Soriano was not at his desk. They were asked if they wanted to leave a number or a message. They didn't. They waited behind the store, leaning against a low branch of a piñon pine. They had a view of both entrances to the parking lot through scrub oak and juniper. They let ten minutes pass, and they tried again. Kathy was successful.

"Detective Soriano, we got kidnapped!" Kathy went straight to the point.

"At the restaurant?"

"No…we weren't at a restaurant. He took us to his house and pulled a gun on us and made us get into the trunk of his car."

"Who?"

"Your partner, Officer Probasco, he's part of the posse."

"Detective Probasco called and told me you wanted to eat and get your stuff later. You need to come in to my office and clear things up. The computer jump stick was blank. I need to know what's going on."

"Blank?"

"Yes, blank as in empty. You need to come in."

"We can't come in right now because we are running again. We don't feel safe. This is awful. He was taking us to the posse to beat information out of us. He hit Jerry in the head. I think they are going to kill us," Kathy said.

"You have to stop running away. It makes you look guilty. You have to admit this does not look good. I want to help you. Where are you? I'll send a squad car to pick you up."

"We can't stay anywhere with police protection. We... you, don't know who is and who is not a member of the posse. We don't know what to do. You didn't even know Probasco was one of them. How can you assure us we will be safe?" Kathy spelled out the dilemma in the best way she could under all the stress.

"Detective Probasco has been a friend for many years. I know him. I trust him. I think your recent experience is causing you to see things that are not there. You've been through a lot. Now where are you? I'll come and get you myself." Soriano sounded exasperated, and it came across as slightly angry.

Jerry moved carefully to Kathy, "I think we need to go. I see a man searching over there on the hill, and he's coming this way. Kathy hung up, and they slipped around the shop, and Jerry angled away using the building as a blind. They hustled past the Three Scotsmen Rock formation and then turned northwest into thicker foliage. They zigzagged around clumps of pine and rock.

"What should we do now?" Kathy asked.

"I think we should circle around and get back into town. What did Detective Soriano say?"

"He said the jump drive was blank."

"Blank!"

"Yes, blank and he wants us to come in now. He didn't believe me when I told him what Probasco did to us. He trusts him. Probasco told him that we wanted to eat at a restaurant and he dropped us off."

Jerry's mind was only half on what Kathy was saying and the other on the blank drive. "Probasco did that to us too."

"You mean the drive?"

"Yes, it's the only explanation. He had to erase it after he took it from the conference room. I double-checked it to make sure it was a good copy. Kathy, do you think Soriano is one of them?"

"I don't know. Sometimes he sounded like he believed me, and at other times he sounded like he trusts Probasco and wants us to come in. I'm worried. We are not safe in either scenario."

"The pictures are our only proof. We have to get to them and give him or someone else another copy. I made several." They were ascending a loose gravel hill and the effort to climb was slowing progress. "We need to get on solid ground. Even a toddler could follow us in this."

"Sir, they went to the store and then are heading north, ah, west north. Their tracks are easy to follow," Bradley spoke over the phone.

"Good, I'll call in some more men. It looks like they're headed back into the mountains toward Waldo Canyon. Keep me informed." Webber hung up and called his second in charge. He told him what had happened and what he needed. His mind was arranging priorities. The money was important, but remaining innocent in the eyes of the police was more important. He had to discredit the two soldiers and get them out of the way. If they disappeared altogether it would look as if they were guilty and running from the law. He was beginning to discount the need of retrieving the money in favor of maintaining the status quo. He instructed his assistant commander to have the guys ready for the field with full equipment. He reminded him they were on a manhunt to terminate. He called the men, one by one, who were already on the chase and told them to close on Bradley because he was on the trail.

He waited for the ambulance to arrive to take Probasco to the hospital.

Soriano was in consternation. The case of two car thieves, supposedly rampaging soldiers, had grown into a huge conspiracy involving leading members of the force. Pictures proving the story were nonexistent, and the informers had turned-tail and run. He was angry with his partner, and he had to call him to find the truth. He hit speed dial. No answer, just voicemail. He waited and tried again. This time he got an unfamiliar voice.

"This is Mr. Probasco's phone, can I help you?"

"Who is this?"

"I'm an emergency medical technician. My name is Barry. Are you a relative of Mr. Probasco?"

"I'm his partner, Detective Soriano. What's happened?"

"I can't give you any details over the phone, but I am at liberty to tell you he has been in an auto accident, and we are bringing him to Penrose Hospital. Can you contact his family for him?"

"Yes, I can do that." Officer Soriano ended the conversation and called his friend's wife. He told her he would be along to visit as soon as he cleared things up. He hung up and rubbed his temples to relieve the headache that was building. His get-it-done work ethic was stymied. He needed more information. He almost rushed to the hospital, but then he thought of the pictures. He called Preston.

"Preston, any luck with the jump stick?"

"A little. It has been erased. I've been able to reconstruct small bits. It's not much. You can come down and see what I have." The detective took his coat and went straight to the lab. He placed his hands on the back of Preston's chair and stared. He leaned forward as if he could clarify the dots and squares by being closer to the screen. The fragment gave the impression of a faraway panorama of flat open space. No men with guns.

"Do you have anything else?"

"This." Preston hit a key. The pixels seemed to float on a sea of white. A cluster gave the faint idea of a pine needle with a cone attached close by.

"I can tell there used to be a video and that is much harder to reconstruct. I'm afraid that's all I have."

"Thanks for your work." Soriano took another look at the screen and left for the hospital.

The front range of the Rockies rises up from the prairie like a dam holding back invisible water. Jerry and Kathy were edging on the Rampart Range at Waldo Canyon adjacent to Colorado Springs to the east and fourteen-thousand-foot Pikes Peak to the southwest. Their visibility over the ground behind them was superb.

"Jerry, we've got less to work with than last time. We don't have binoculars or water or a first aid kit."

"We have a gun to fight back this time. We didn't have that for most of last time. And, we have my trusty card knife." Jerry focused on the positive. Kathy pulled the knife out of her pullover pocket.

"This was a surprise. Where did you get it?" she said, holding the small knife.

"Chuck gave it to me. He gave it to several of the guys. It was one of those recruiting incentives for his citizen militia. I thought it was a pretty cool gadget but didn't know if I would ever use it."

"Well, it saved our lives," Kathy observed.

"When we crest this rise, we can start to our right and try to come back down. We need to hide our trail, so let's keep on the lookout for hard surfaces that won't show our direction," he instructed.

"You got it, gadget man."

The evening sun hid behind the ridge. It was hours before official sunset, but the barrier of the mountains cast a shadow over the east side of the Front Range. What they found over the rise was the beginning of a gully running down to the left. Ahead was the burnt area of the Waldo Canyon fire. The charred trees would not give them cover. They adjusted their plans to go down the gully. Jerry wanted to create a ruse and lead them up and away. He searched for the appropriate material, a fallen log or a flat rock to disguise foot prints. To the left and up a hundred feet was a large tree with a dead one lying on the ground pointing uphill. They climbed up the scree past the tree, went past the log ten paces, and then backtracked again in the same footfalls. They stepped onto the fallen log, followed it back to the tree, climbed the tree and went out on a limb and lowered themselves to scattered stones on the ground. Tip toeing on stones they angled to a large flat stone and ran along it to the gulley. They concentrated on their steps and made sure any marks they left were not discernible to the human eye. After a mile they felt comfortable talking again.

"How did you learn this stuff?" she asked.

"What stuff?" he answered.

"The way you know how to hide our tracks. They didn't teach this in basic."

"I read it in the book, *Where the Red Fern Grows*. In there, it's a raccoon that hides his trail."

"I see, so you learn from fictional animals," Kathy teased.

"More or less."

"In the book, did the raccoon walk backward on its own foot prints?"

"No, I made that one up on my own."

"I thought so," Kathy replied.

The gully was easier to move down, and they made good time. They were headed for Fountain Creek less than a mile away and had a clear view of HWY 24. They watched for any cars familiar to the ones they had seen the first day. In the late afternoon it was a busy highway, people heading out of the city for houses in the hills. To their left toward Colorado Springs there was open area with some businesses along the highway. To their right, foliage carpeted the shoulder of the small mountain they sat upon. They wanted concealment and chose the longer route to the right away from town paralleling Fountain Creek. They had to dodge around the attractions of Manitou Indian Cliff Dwellings and the larger Cave of the Winds. They were about to duck under the highway to the other side after using a bridge over a small stream when they saw a red four-by-four parked on the opposite side. It had a man standing next to it glassing the ground they were covering with high-powered field glasses. They couldn't continue in his direction; it was too risky. They slunk up the hill, using the heavy cover.

Bradley kept to the trail even though his concentration was interrupted by repeated phone calls. The calls were coming from Webber, who was directing his troops. He had a map on his lap and followed Bradley's every move. He cordoned off the couple by sending men up side roads, highways, and creek beds. He had sentinels at strategic locations. Bradley whooped when he saw the clear marks ascending alongside the fallen tree. He ran up the hill even though the exertion made his head spin. His head was not completely right after the clobbering he had received in the stable. He slowed down and kept climbing.

After a couple hundred yards, he could not discern a trail. He cast to the right, then the left. He moved up and did the same. He had to come back. He cut the distance to the last track by half and cast in left and right patterns. He was doing what he did when he had tracked wounded game following a blood trail. He had to sit down because his head hurt too much. Another phone call came. He explained he was trying to pick up the trail that had gone cold. Webber asked him to call back as soon as he found it. It took half an hour to seek both sides before returning to the tracks above the tree. This was it, the end of the trail. Stupidly he looked up as if they had gone into the sky. He knew that couldn't be it. He asked himself, *what would I do if I knew I was being followed?* His head ached. *Change direction, that's what I would do.* Bradley got up slowly to avoid falling over. He went right and found soft gravel and reddish dirt. No tracks. Then he went left downhill, and in the gulley he found a partial footprint. It matched one of their hiking boots. He called Webber.

Webber then swiftly concentrated his force to the Fountain Creek drainage. The fellows he sent up Rampart Range Road he called back. The noose was tightening. He would get them soon.

⌘

Soriano showed his badge at the emergency entrance and walked to the trauma room where Probasco was being treated. Mrs. Probasco was there. His long-time friend was in the CT scan room. He comforted her in the best way he could. "Is he going to be all right?"

"Yes, they say he should make a full recovery."

"Good, I'm glad. Do they know what happened?"

"They said he hit his head when the car went off the road."

"Does anyone know why he ran off the road? Was it another car in the wrong lane or a drunk driver?"

"They don't know. The nurse said he was found by a passerby who called it in."

"Is he talking? Did you get a chance to see him?"

"Yes, I got here just when they were wheeling him to the CT room. He seems confused and groggy, just like after his surgery two years ago. Thanks for calling me. I was getting ready to leave work and go cook supper."

Detective Soriano waited for Probasco to return. He wondered if he could get some answers. Fifteen minutes later they brought him back, the trauma surgeon followed the technicians and nurses as they reconnected him to the monitors. The surgeon explained the damage.

"He has suffered a severe blow to his front cranium. They are some hairline fractures that will need to heal. He has a significant concussion, and we will want to admit him for observation. The good thing is, I can't see any bleeding inside. But we'll watch for that too with more CT scans. It would be helpful if you kept the lights low and loud music from playing." The surgeon excused himself and went to dictate his report.

His wife held his hand. He saw Detective Soriano, and his eyes opened wider.

"What happened, old friend?" Soriano began.

"I guess I hit a tree. I can't remember very much." Probasco was cognizant enough to know what Webber had set up as a cover. He also exaggerated his fuzzy condition. He didn't want to face questions and answers from a trained detective. He felt at a disadvantage. He turned and spoke to his wife. "Don't worry, honey. I'll...be all right."

Soriano stayed around for more small talk, hoping a better conversation might erupt. He would not ask any probing question and spill the beans about what Kathy had said about him on the phone. He found it difficult to believe, yet disturbing. He wondered if his friend might start saying something.

※※※

"Kathy, I didn't see any police cars on the road. Neither going nor coming. The man following us at the shop was not in a uniform, and the one across the highway was not in a uniform. I think maybe the posse is handling this by themselves. What do you think?"

"I see what you're saying. I'm sorry my mind was working on 'what ifs,'" she apologized.

"Like what kind of 'what ifs?'"

"Well, what if the posse is really big, and what if they are everywhere and in my hometown asking my parents questions, and what if we will never get away from them?"

Jerry wanted to comfort her in some way. "I think you're worrying outside the box. I want to focus on the here and now and solve that before I move on to your bigger what ifs. It helps me to keep my purpose simple."

"So you want to KISS," she asked pointedly.

"What?" Jerry's eyebrows shot up.

"You know, KISS—keep it simple, stupid."

"You got it. It works for me 'cause I'm stupid."

"You are not stupid! You're a very bright compassionate man. I'd go with you anywhere." Kathy bit her lip too late. She wondered if she had said too much. "You're right, we should focus on what's happening now. Later we can talk about my 'what ifs.'"

"I'm thinking we need to stay on this side of the road until we have another opportunity to cross over that highway and double back into town."

"Maybe we'll have to wait until dark." Kathy was into the box and working the near issue.

"All right, but we still need to keep adding up the miles in case they're following close. That guy did a good job of finding us at the stable." Jerry ducked under a limb and headed for a ridge that would hide them from view with solid ground rather than porous soil and scant plant life covering their passage. Their path paralleled the highway and ran beside the little community of Cascade. Not more than two dozen buildings occupied the ground alongside Fountain Creek. They couldn't risk moving through an area where watchers could be in parked cars. On the opposite side they could see a paved road heading up toward Pikes Peak.

"I wish we could walk on paved road. They would not be able to follow us very easily. The trick is getting on it without them seeing where we did," Jerry wished. Two miles further up the state highway they could see Chipita Park, slightly bigger than Cascade. Jerry got an idea. He swung down into the valley and slid into a deep ravine, and they crossed under the highway by crawling through a culvert. On the other side they walked up town roads in the darkening light. On the south side of the village where the roads turned to gravel, he told Kathy to take off her fleece jacket, as he did his. Then she watched as he wrapped his on his right foot and hers on his left foot and tied them on.

He turned his back toward her and said "Hop on." She had to smile at his ingenuity. Jerry's feet left no distinguishable marks even though he was a hundred pounds heavier. He did the fireman's carry up the dirt road, passing many turn offs and onto the paved Pikes Peak road. Kathy could see the small maze of residential roads they had passed would multiply the followers' problems.

On the paved road they took the jackets off his feet and walked back down the other side of the Fountain Creek drainage. They came to a bend with a view down toward the valley and the lights of the city that were just coming on. It was the escape back into town that they wanted. They knelt behind the guardrail to scan the terrain. There on the road below them, three cars were parked and a conference was taking place. One of the cars was the red four-by-four they had seen before with the man and his binoculars. As they watched, two men slipped into the trees, blocking their path down to the city. They had to back track up the road.

They turned to slide away from the guardrail when a vehicle came up the road. They were exposed on the road-side of the guardrail away from the downside where the men had concluded their conference. They were caught in between. They had seconds to decide what to do. They could stand and walk normally in hopes the driver was not posse, but then they would be exposed to the eyes of the observer by the SUV below. Soon they would be illuminated.

"Jerry, get down! We can't take a chance." They both flattened themselves on the ground next to the guardrail and then rolled underneath to the other side. They were two living logs in beige and brown fleece, suspended in animation, hoping not to be discovered, lying in plain sight from the observer below. They buried their faces in the dirt. The vehicle approached and slowed at the turn, coming to a stop parallel to the barrier. It sat with the motor running two feet from their prone bodies, using the same vantage point for viewing the valley. Jerry could see the wheels and the lower portion of the door panels. It was a black SUV. If he wanted to he could reach out and touch the rocker panel.

He didn't move. Static from a walkie-talkie crackled and then stopped in favor of a voice.

"Commander, this is Jackson. It's getting darker, and we are losing visibility. We need those scopes. What do you advise?"

"The scopes are coming. Stay where you are and watch for moving shadows or listen for noises. They will think the night will hide their movements. We might catch them when they move. Be alert."

"Roger."

A cigarette stub was tossed out of the driver's side window and it landed on Jerry's upper arm. It smoldered in his sleeve. Slowly, very slowly, he twisted his arm to let the butt fall to the ground. Part of his sleeve glowed from the hot ashes that ignited the fibers. He could feel the heat as it burned its way to his flesh. He needed to pat the area and smother it, but could not risk sudden movement. He rolled his arm uncomfortably as far as the joint would allow. If it had landed on his forearm, it would have been better. It was just above his elbow. Twisting his shoulders at glacial speed, he was able to press the fabric against the dirt. It served to press the burning fibers into his arm, searing his flesh.

"Commander calling Bradley, come in Bradley."

"Yes, sir."

"Where are you, and tell me what you know."

"I'm in Chapita Park. They came here from under the highway, and I've lost their trail. They may have gone into one of the houses."

"I doubt that. Officer Barns, on my command, has gone through the town, warning everyone to lock their doors, sheds, and cars. He's down there now watching the main road on the west side."

"What should I do?"

"Keep looking for a trail, but work your way east toward me. I'm on the forest road leading to the reservoir. I'll wait for you."

"Yes, sir."

Jerry wanted to have the revolver in his hand, but it was pinned beneath him, stuck in his belt. Moving to smother the cigarette burn was risky enough. He couldn't risk any more movement. He was so close he could hear Webber munching on peanuts as he used binoculars to scan the hillside and the slope leading to the posse member below them. If he chose to get out for any reason, he would be able to see their forms lying at his feet. Time oozed by like honey in a freezer. Every sound seemed amplified. Every stick, stone, and pebble was making impressions upon their skin. The service revolver felt like a six-by-six board jammed into Jerry's stomach. Kathy grew cold with anxiety, shivering was not an option, so she clinched her teeth. She planned to grab the little knife if any change in their status developed.

An empty plastic peanut bag floated down upon them, thrown from the window. After some audible gulps from a water bottle, Lieutenant Webber started to hack out a cough. Some of the water must have trickled down his windpipe. With a few sips of water, the commander was able to control his cough and then clear his throat. He spat out a glob of phlegm that landed on Kathy's head next to her ear. Every ounce of restraint was mustered to keep from jumping up and screaming her disgust. She couldn't even shudder in bodily protest. Her skin crawled, and her toes scrunched into a ball inside her hiking boots.

Gravel could be heard scrunching under boots at the road's edge. Someone was walking slowly up the road toward their position. Looking under the SUV, Jerry could see a shadow against the dim lights filtering through the trees from the town of Chapita Park. Every few steps the shadow would pause by the side of the woods. Then it would move on. Sometimes it would stop, backtrack a step or two, and then come forward. Jerry watched as the shadow drew nearer. It had to be Bradley coming to his commander. Jerry prayed that he would stay on the other side of the four-by-four. As the foot falls came closer, he could almost make out the type of boots. Across the road Bradley walked toward the parked vehicle, and then suddenly he changed course and went to the front of the SUV swinging around to the driver's side and walking between the guardrail barrier and his commander's car. He sat on the barrier and began to talk into the window. Kathy could have stabbed him in the butt at only a foot and a half away. She could have cut the strings off his boots. These thoughts and others flitted through her mind.

"Where do you think they are?" Webber asked.

"They have to be somewhere near. Their tracks came into this area. They can't be far away."

"I'll bring in men to watch all the roads and trails. We'll seal up this valley and catch them in our net. I sent Rutherford to get the night scopes. Damn! I wish I'd thought of that earlier. I thought we had them."

"We'll get 'em, sir."

"Get in. I need to pick up Rogers and Jacobs and bring them back here."

The soldiers nervously inhaled when Bradley stood. He walked around the front and turned his head down to check for prints in the loose gravel by the rail.

"Step on it, Bradley. There's nothing here. I've checked." The lights came on and illuminated the landscape. The gearshift clicked, and a door opened and slammed shut. Webber turned the wheels sharply and drove back down the main road.

The pair remained like log statues for several minutes then rolled out under and away from the rail. On hands and knees they groped along the ground to the end of the rail and slunk into the woods. As soon as they were out of sight, Kathy went into gyrations, acting as if a hornet had crawled into her ear. She grabbed her hair and cleaned off the glop and then snatched leaves to wipe off the rest and then ripped more off of branches to clean her hands. She still didn't feel clean.

"We've got to get out of here fast before they get their scopes!" Jerry whispered.

"Which way?"

"The only way I can see is up this road until we get out of their trap," he answered. They stayed in the woods and followed the road for several hundred yards. They were making too much noise stepping on unseen twigs and stumbling over rocks and roots. They mutually decided to use the hard top road and keep sound discipline in favor of stealth. Their eyes and ears would be the cover.

They kept to the road beyond where they had acquired it and moved northwest. Pikes Peak was to their left, a massive mountain guiding them further into the woods and into more rugged terrain. The road took them to and around a reservoir. They saw the name posted on a sign: "Crystal Creek Reservoir." A feeder stream enabled them to get drinks and Kathy thoroughly washed her hair attempting decontamination. They drank as much as they could hold, not knowing when the next water source would replenish them.

Darkness surrounded them. It was infinitely easier to walk on the road instead of through forest brush and trees. It felt like it was an evening stroll, only worries inhabited their thoughts. The road inclined higher and higher, at one point the moon elevated from behind Pikes Peak and illuminated the countryside. They were leery of being bathed in moonlight and needed to get out of sight. Jerry sought the best place to disguise their exit off the paved road. He found a log jam of fallen trees and took them like an elevated sidewalk. They slipped off the last log and toward a flickering campfire light below. With the police out of the hunt, they felt the posse might not have every base covered. If there was a campfire, there might be a campground; if there was a campground, there may be some potable water. They needed water more than food, even though their stomachs felt like shriveled raisins. The silent night with lunar light encouraged silent movement. No nocturnal beast would have known they were near. Late evening they approach the fire. There were several fires, but the one they could see was on their side of the campground. They crouched in the bushes, watching and listening. Happy excited talk could be heard—children roasting marshmallows and adults telling stories by the fire. Jerry listened then spoke.

"That's what I wanted to do with, well…you know… Go camping and watch my kids poke sticks in the fire and make them burn."

"See, you have good dreams too." Kathy rubbed his back in empathy. "Did you do a lot of camping when you were growing up?"

"Yes," he said thoughtfully.

"What was your favorite camping trip?"

"Yellowstone," he said without hesitation. "We went to Yellowstone and camped near Fisherman's Bridge. Every day I went to the bridge and caught my limit and Mom would fry them, and I felt like the big man providing for the family. Sea gulls were flying everywhere making noise and calling to each other. They were really noisy when I cleaned the fish. They must have told every gull in the neighborhood what I was doing, because there were hundreds of them trying to get the fish guts. I ended up having fun throwing the innards into the air and watching them dive and catch them and eat them." Kathy cringed at the thought of guts flying in the air, but didn't say anything.

"Did you like seeing the geysers?" she prodded.

"Oh, yes. That was nice. But I liked the time at night with the family talking about unimportant stuff. Now, they only talk of their political opinions and their anti-war stance. I wish we could go back to that happy time."

"And you wanted to recreate that happy life with a wife and kids?"

Jerry took in a heavy breath and let it go out his nose. "Yes, that's what I wanted."

"Someday that will happen for you," Kathy encouraged.

Kathy looked at her watch. It said eleven thirty. Her eyes were tired, and she remembered they had arisen near 6 a.m. She wanted to sleep. The fires started to die out, and parents put kids into the tents and campers. Another ten minutes and embers were the only glow in the camp. Kathy and Jerry felt it was safe to move in on the pump and get fresh water.

After drinking bellies full, they headed off into the woods. They both searched for a place to sleep. Jerry found a large tree with extensive roots and smaller shrubs covering the ground over the roots. Aspen leaves had collected in between the roots, blown there from last fall. A green pine bough lay broken on the ground a casualty from a windstorm or lightning. With his hand, he pushed a pile of leaves into one large root cavity and asked for Kathy to lie down, and then he said, "We'll have to share body heat," and without preamble lay beside her. They rustled leaves over them, and Jerry pulled the pine bough on top. It was reasonably comfortable considering the Spartan nature of the materials. She pulled his arm over her and snuggled into his body backward. She then took her arms out of her jacket sleeves and folded them in front of her chest. Slumber arrived in minutes.

CHAPTER 6

"Jerry, your hands and arms are cold. Put them under my jacket with mine. Mine are warm." When he complied she held both his hands and clutched them in an effort to warm them. It settled them enough to put them back to sleep for another couple of hours. The rest was necessary for their fight. It was a defensive weapon protecting them from making uncalculated decisions and strengthening them for more physical exertion. Lying in a tight spot with little room to move caused their joints to stiffen. It took some stretching to limber up and start the journey. The cold morning air could be seen in light little puffs of breath. No preparation was necessary. No packs to be packed and hefted. No clothes had to be put on and zipped up. They stood up and walked, and walking felt vital as it brought heat to their cold muscles.

Their aim was Colorado Springs, but Pikes Peak hindered any direct passageway to what little possessions they had in downtown storage. They needed the basics but had only the clothes on their backs. Instead of going straight up and over, they had to skirt along the wide shoulder. They didn't know what was ahead; Jerry had never seen a map of this territory before. They dead-reckoned, always keeping the dominating peak on the left shoulder. Hunger clawed inside and threatened to climb up their throats. Water came at regular intervals from streams and small rills. They drank at every opportunity.

"We've got to eat!" Jerry remarked suddenly.

"No argument there. Know of a nice bistro nearby?" Kathy quipped.

"As a matter of fact I do." Jerry stopped near a sapling pine. It was early enough in the season for the new growth tips to be lighter green than the rest of the needles. He plucked a couple and put them in his mouth. "I've heard about this but have never tried it before. Ah…not too bad." He chewed slowly and pulled off a couple more. Kathy watched. Then, because he was eating, she felt that she could at least give it a try. She took a few nibbles.

"Okay, if my stable oats go with blueberry yogurt, what do your pine needles go with?"

"A nice vinaigrette would help and maybe some dried cranberries. What would you suggest, my gourmand?"

"If I'm a gourmand, then you're a forest epicure. Do you have any other woodland dishes for our consumption?"

"We could dine on cattails and cactus. For protein some earthworms would do nicely," Jerry suggested between bites.

"How exactly do you eat earthworms?"

"Live, of course. I've tried them filleted, but they still wiggle a bunch." Jerry smirked. Kathy shuddered.

"Okay, that did it! I don't think I'm hungry anymore."

"Me neither. I'm going to wait for lunch at the five-star Broadmoor Hotel," Jerry dreamt.

"That sounds nice. Do you need conversational company?" Kathy offered.

"It would be my pleasure to have your company at my table." Jerry bowed.

※※

Morning mist clung to the valleys. The sun had not burned it away because it was still straining to heave itself over the landmass blocking the way. At eleven thousand feet, the air was crisp. The sentinel blew warm air into his gloves and repositioned the binoculars to his eyes. He checked the open areas for movement. He felt it was useless to keep searching. They had lost the trail.

The night before, Bradley had followed them down to Chipita Park. The men tried looking at all the roads leading away and looking for disturbed markings. Webber decided to deploy his men at vantage points along the valley and up high on the sides of hills and mountains. They settled into positions before sun up after a solid night's sleep in warm, comfortable beds.

The low-lying cloud layer was only a temporary disadvantage. Above, the sky was pure and clean. The lookout situated himself on a fallen spruce below and to the west of a sharp ridge appropriately named, Sentinel Point. He waited. He was the last lookout in the line Webber had set up. He could see a number of lakes and reservoirs scattered across the skirts of the mountain. Streams ran off the mountain like thin ribbons of blue. The sun was almost to his position, and he awaited the warming rays.

Since the couple was running crosswise to descending mountain ravines, the trek was up and down like a rollercoaster ride. The rise to the left and the decline to their right gave the direction they needed. Here and there blue sky shined through scattering clouds. It was almost miraculous the way the haze rapidly disappeared. They grew tense and alert once concealment evaporated. Again they wanted speed to be their ally in putting distance from the pursuit, which they did not know if it still existed.

They came to a treeless expanse where a herd of elk had just vacated. The warm piles of droppings sent little streams of vapor up from where they had been left behind. The duo paused to plan the route. They then dropped lower as they followed the taller shrubbery around the open space.

The sentinel had watched the elk herd disappear into the brush. It was the only movement he could detect in his sector. He knew the elk were settling down for a nap. He marked this spot in his mind as a possible location for hunting season next fall. His binocular-assisted eyes tried to penetrate the surrounding area for good places to set up a blind. He could see beige color moving from right to left and concluded that the herd was searching for concealment. Then he realized it was not the tawny color of elk hide but a beige jacket behind tree trunks moving with a darker brown in front going in the same direction. He immediately called Webber.

The hunt began again. They were spotted heading southeast. Webber brought some men in high scattered across the face of the mountain and some low. The ones on the high ground had high-velocity rifles with scopes. The others circled from roads and trails below. Bradley followed with Webber on the trail they hoped to pick up from the sentinel's mark. They were closing the quarry in a living vice.

About an hour later, the upper arm of the posse had moved into position. They could swiftly cover ground at twelve thousand feet where no trees or shrubbery blocked their advance. Once they were strung out along the mountain, they descended to close the vice. They worked in teams; one watched while the other moved. It was close to noon when a team spotted the pair through some trees. The sniper dropped to a prone position, aimed, and fired. It was a long shot at over eight hundred yards. He figured the targets would panic and run headlong into his teammates.

Without gear they traveled easily on foot; the difficulty came when they had to climb over forest debris. Game trails helped, but the trails usually led to water, which was most always down slope, and to meadows for grazing. And the more lush meadows were open areas, which they wished to avoid. They had to switch on and off the trails. There was one location that had a split in the trees and a trail that led first downhill and then around an outcropping of boulders. Kathy was in the lead, and Jerry followed.

The bullet came straight at Jerry's back and hit him at the same moment he turned to go around the rocks. He stumbled and fell. Kathy heard the report and saw Jerry fall. She panicked, running to him. He lay on the ground on his side.

"I'm hit."

"No, please no!" Kathy begged, falling beside him. "Where? Where are you hurt?"

"My back. I can feel it in two places. It must have been two bullets." Jerry wanted to touch his pain, but it was out of reach. Kathy had tears welling in her eyes as she rolled him facedown partially on her knees. She could see two bullet holes in his pullover, one over each scapula.

"No, not *my* Jerry! It can't be! Please!" She knelt beside him and shoved his jacket up and pulled his shirt out of his pants. Blood washed all over his upper back, masking the extent of his wounds.

"Kathy, it's weird. It doesn't seem bad. I'm breathing. Everything seems…normal inside, I think. I've never been shot before. I don't know what it's supposed to feel like," he said with a touch of panic in his voice.

She wasn't listening to him; she was wiping blood away from what looked like two bullet holes. They were elongated tatters, both of which ran in a single line across his upper back, skipping over the indentation of his spine. Silently she worked to examine the insides of the wounds. It looked like tattered meat, without broken bones. Relief was starting to flood her being. She took the card knife from her pocket and used it to tear strips of her own shirttail to use as bandages. The relief overwhelmed her when she had the bleeding staunched. She dropped onto his back and hugged him, smearing blood on the front of her fleece jacket. "Jerry, Jerry, you're going to be all right! It's okay. I can stop the bleeding." She gave up trying to take small shreds off the bottom of her shirt; instead she stabbed and ripped, taking long strips and patches, using half of the shirt. From those she fashioned pads and crude slings circling his chest and shoulders. She worked fast.

Jerry worried about how he could keep going now that he was injured; he wondered, at first, if it was critical and if he might die. Her hug from behind made him feel responsible for her protection, even though her words were discounted as premature wishful thinking. He felt for the revolver in the pocket of his pullover that was now crumpled around his shoulders and neck. He tried to sit up, which ended up helping Kathy as she wrapped strips around the front of his torso. He didn't feel any restrictions from inside. His breathing was rapid but normal. His head was clear.

She pulled down his shirt and jacket, and he plucked out the revolver. "Run, Kathy, I'll hold them off until you can get away." He moved to his knees to look around a large stone.

"Are you crazy? I'm never leaving you. *Never!*"

"You've got to go. I might not be able to make it very far. But you can. *Run!*"

"Nonsense, you big baby, the bullet just creased your back. It's just bleeding and I have that stopped."

Jerry had to process her words. Calling him a big baby hurt, but it jolted him out of his negative fatalism. "Really?"

"Yes, really. Now, let's both get outta here."

Jerry concentrated. "Okay…I guess we'll both have to run." He looked over the edge of the stone and saw the men who had put him down. His emotions of relief and chagrin were overpowered by welling anger. "First, I'm going to slow them down." He steadied the pistol on the rock and waited. The moment came when one moved forward while the other stayed behind. He aimed for the center of mass and pulled the trigger.

The team immediately reported in their success. "I put one of them down. I got him in the back, and he went down immediately. They're right below us."

"Are you sure?" Webber asked.

"I'm sure. He fell immediately, and they haven't moved."

"Good, I want you to move in on them and signal the rest of the team. We'll close from all sides."

The team gave instructions to their right and left and the others passed on the directions. They moved down the hill in shifts, one watching and the other walking forward. They kept a constant vigil on where they saw him fall, which was at the edge of the rock. They approached within a hundred yards, and the shot came from the stones to the left of the kill site. It hit his right lung, and the surprise threw him back on his posterior. He clutched his chest, willing the wound to magically disappear. He tried to sit up and reacquire his rifle, thinking he could fight back. His right arm would not obey his commands, and his breathing was coming in labored rasps. His wild eyes were aware of his dilemma before his mind could accept the facts.

His partner crawled to him and dragged him back to cover and started administering first-aid. It took a few moments for them to call in the new development.

"Okay, now we can run," Jerry instructed. They hustled bent over into the woods in the same direction as before. They were silent. The course they took was not thought out; just by repetition they kept going. After a hundred yards, they questioned why.

"Kathy, I'm thinking our plan to go around the mountain may not be the best. They found us, and they might be ahead of us. Maybe they were watching us before they shot me," Jerry whispered.

"If we go back, there might be more of them back there. It's scary any way we go," she answered.

"If we keep going in the same general direction but stay to the thicker trees and cover, we might have a chance."

"Okay." They moved down slope into heavier foliage. Their progress was greatly slowed by obstacles and slow stealthy movement. They were alert, thinking and planning tactically. They came to a clearing that forced them to make calculations. They lay on the ground and peered from beneath ferns.

"How's your back? Does it hurt?" Kathy spoke softly.

"It's okay. It still stings a bunch."

"Here let me take a look." Jerry rolled away and Kathy pushed up his clothes. The makeshift bandages were soaked. She cut off some more of her shirt and slid the folded pads under the others. She could see the edges of the wounds were starting to crystallize.

"Ah, I hope you weren't planning on being a shirtless male model. You'll probably end up with some nasty scars."

"Nope, being a model was not on my list," he said. Kathy smiled, then she had an overwhelming feeling she should do some explaining.

"Back there I thought you were going to die. It really scared me." Jerry turned to look at her. "I need to say something and it has to be now," she demanded.

"All right."

"I didn't want to come home from Afghanistan," she announced. Jerry became curious. "Coming home meant I would no longer be able to see you every day. My heart was heavy, and I couldn't tell you how I felt. You know because…it wouldn't be fair to you. It's different now. A little while ago, I thought you might die and I would never have the chance to tell you how much you mean to me. I was really, really afraid you would die thinking that no one loves you as much as I do. I can't go another day, another moment, with you not knowing. You don't have to say you love me too, because that is not why I am saying this. I just don't want the man I adore to be alone in his heart." Tears cascaded off her cheeks.

Jerry put his arm over her in a one-arm hug, comforting her. She turned toward him, embracing him with both her arms. He reciprocated, and they lay there quietly holding each other as if they were on a blanket in a warm sunny park on a Memorial Day afternoon.

"I don't know what to say..." Jerry hesitated.

"I don't want you to say anything that is not true." She held her fingertips to his lips. He waited.

"This past year has been good and bad for me; bad, because I was so far away from Sharon, good because I had you as a friend. Believe me when I say, many times I have had thoughts about you, but I put them away because I wanted to be true to Sharon. Sometimes I could not get you out of my head, and I would feel guilty about it. Now, I...well..."

"Don't say it." Jerry stopped when she said that. They were so close their noses were almost touching. "Jerry, what you said just now makes me admire you all the more. You are a man of integrity. You stayed true to Sharon in your head thousands of miles away. I will wait forever for your thoughts to settle about Sharon. I'll be waiting patiently. I don't want you to rush."

"Question."

"Go ahead," she said with a little curiosity.

"You said, 'My Jerry.' Was that a slip?"

"Yes, it was." Kathy looked a little embarrassed.

"I'll make a deal with you. I will be your Jerry if you will agree to be my Kathy." Jerry peered deep into her eyes, and her eyes kept looking from one to another of his. She saw his honesty, and she saw more than she ever had hoped for in Afghanistan. "Yes, I'd like that." A breeze in the trees caused them to refocus; they shifted back to side-by-side and watched the field before them. They were closer than before; closer in spirit.

They settled on moving back up and then around to the other side of the meadow undercover. It meant traveling three times farther. On the other side, they stopped and watched behind them. It was an excellent place to see if they were being followed.

"I guess we answered one of your 'what ifs,'" Jerry opined.

"The what if we have to shoot them, 'what if?'"

"Yes."

"Did you?" Kathy tentatively asked.

"I shot him. Hit him in the middle of the chest."

"How did you feel about it?"

"I felt anger, because he shot me, and good that I got him back. Before that, I felt I needed to protect you because he was coming to finish us off. He had his weapon at his hip ready to fire again if he saw us."

"I see. I think I felt the same way when I hit that guy with the shovel. I was protecting you, and I was very angry when he shot at you," Kathy said.

"I think they have changed their tactics. They're shooting to kill, which I think means they are more interested in getting rid of us than getting the money back," Jerry explained.

"It changes things, doesn't it?"

"Yes, it does. We are now in full self-defense mode."

They were talking and hushed quickly when they saw two posse members come out of the woods. One had a rifle strapped over his shoulder and a walkie-talkie to his ear. The other grasped a handgun at his side. It was time to leave. They traveled as fast as they could up and away from their pursuers. They edged upon another open space to their left. They could see two more coming down at an angle straight at their present location. They felt the noose closing around them. They ran. Zigzagging through trees and underbrush, they came to another open field. They had to cross it as fast as possible before the posse reached the same spot and could see them. They sprinted.

Behind them, gunshots were fired. Bullets ripped the air above and to one side of them. They were spotted. The sanctuary of the trees embraced them. Jerry stood beside a pine on the verge of the open area. He watched for movement and picked out a boulder in the near vicinity of where he thought the bullets had come from. The enemy kept to the cover. He carefully aimed at the boulder and squeezed the trigger. The report was one deterrent, the zing of a ricochet another added preventative. The reports of the return fire came from near the boulder. He shot twice more.

They moved to their right downhill, and Jerry shot again twice, giving the impression there were two armed and firing. He didn't waste time watching for a reaction. He let them think they were going to continue to fire. He turned on the speed and followed Kathy deeper into the woodland. Return fire came sporadically.

They added another half mile to the distance they already had on the posse. Jerry kept watching his surroundings. They were on a deer trail, moving at almost a run, whereas the pursuers had to be wary about running headlong into an ambush. They were much slower. Jerry found what looked like a perfect set-up. A sizeable log leaned against a tree. He lifted it to see if it was free then put it back down. He cast about for a loose pole. He found it and leaned it up against the log. Kathy asked what she could do, and he told her he needed a stick about three feet long. He found a round rock and brought it to the upper side of the slanted trail. He then positioned the rock on the top of the slant where it would roll if not propped. Kathy had a branch about an inch thick and a little over two feet in length. Jerry carefully placed it under the edge of the rock, making the rock balance on top of the stick. Then he braced the pole on top of the rock and slanted it up to the log. The last act in the preparation was to shift the log's weight partly onto the pole. When the rock was disturbed by something hitting the stick, it would roll out from under the pole, which would start the log falling on the trail. It was the best he could do without a shovel or a wire or string. Kathy looked at the contraption.

"Will it hit one of them when it falls?"

"That's the most I could hope for. What I'm counting on is that it will communicate to them we are setting traps and they have to slow down. Our only advantage is speed." With that they took off at a jog. They moved in and out of gullies and over small hills between drainages.

They were being pushed to a shoulder of the mountain. From above, behind, and below, the posse closed in. A sizeable plateau faced them. All the formations of rocks in this one area topped out at the same level with spaces and gaps in random patterns, crisscrossing the field. They slipped down into the fissures and progressed across. Halfway across they stopped to observe. They looked back and found no movement; nothing from above except wide-open tundra, they could not see over the formation to the reaches below. They were about to move forward and thought to check the ground on the avenue of advance. In the far distance, they could see movement. It was too far to make out close details, like gun barrels or binoculars, but the angle of movement meant hostile intent. It had to be members of the posse. Their only recourse was to check out the downhill edge of the rock formation. They broke out on a ledge overlooking a cliff. They were trapped.

Jerry watched for movement below to the south and to the north. It was only a matter of time before they would be caught. He couldn't hold them all off with the bullets he had left. Kathy looked at him with questioning eyes. He had to find a way. He crawled on his belly to the edge of the cliff to find a way down. Instead, he found an inward angling wall ending in a stream that appeared to be an elongated lake. The stream had flowed in a wide curve against the base of the cliff, probably a reason the overhang existed, the result of a thousand years of erosion. The cliff angled back against their perch. Climbing down meant hanging under an overhang. They were not skilled in basic rock climbing; this would require safety ropes and experience. He dropped a stone into the water. It plunked and sank out of sight.

"We're going to have to jump."

"You've got to be kidding!" Kathy spurted out her words.

"It's us jumping or they capture us. I don't see any other choice."

I've never even jumped off of a high diving board!" she put in plain words. Jerry just waited. She was weighing the circumstances. "What if we break our legs, then we'll really be screwed." Jerry didn't answer. Kathy walked boldly out to the edge and looked downward. It didn't help. The distance was three times that of a deck dive for an Olympian. For these two, it represented a free fall out of control.

"If it will help at all, I'll hold your hand." Jerry stood up and grabbed her hand.

"Any advice before I change my mind?" Kathy asked.

"If you bring your knees up to your chest just before you hit the water, it'll make a neat splash."

"Thanks. That's a great help," Kathy said sarcastically.

"Actually, it *is* a great help. Instead of knifing into the water with your feet, you should splash like a cannonball and you won't go as deep. It's safer that way," Jerry instructed. Kathy listened but didn't answer. She was spooling up her courage for the jump. She took the first audacious step. Three steps later, they plunged off the lip of the rock.

The extended drop took their breath away. Their hearts beat faster than a humming bird. Jerry's hand was turning purple because Kathy's was white from squeezing his. What seemed like years later, they hit the water and the bottom a second after. Kathy had taken Jerry's advice and tried to pull her legs up. Jerry got his knees up a little further. The bottom was a jumble of slippery boulders and angular rocks. The one and only sensation they felt was the bitter sting of frigid water. It was like a brain freeze all over their bodies. The numbing pain clamped onto every muscle, locking them into rigidity. When they surfaced, their lungs could not draw a breath. Tiny specks of air entered and exited their mouths in fleeting little gasps. The scary jump was instantly replaced by hyperventilating hysteria.

The wall next to the cliff was smooth and the opposite side too open and exposed. They went with the current as it pushed them out of the stretched-out lake into the roiling stream. The water pushed them down a cascade like debris in a tidal wave. Hundreds of yards later, they could take no more and had to get out of the water. They rolled onto a muddy bank under a thick mass of willows. The bank was moist from icy runoff of melted snow from alpine packs. The flow of the creek was diminished from days and weeks before. They had a secret sanctuary. Immediately they pulled off the fleece jackets, twisting them to wring out the water after they had emptied the pockets of the knife and revolver. Kathy's shirt looked like the tattered version of a castaway's costume on a postage-stamp-sized island in the Pacific. It barely reached to the point of covering her white lacy bra. Jerry noticed and respectfully did not gawk. Her skin was a mass of goose bumps, and she shivered like a paint-mixing machine. Jerry took his shirt off and wrung out every drop.

"You'll need to take what's left of your shirt off," he whispered. Kathy complied. She started to wring hers out and Jerry put his shirt on her. She didn't protest. She was next to passing out from the cold. He dressed her in her jacket and said, "Now, you'll have to take off those jeans." Still no protest came from her lips. First he unlaced and removed the boots then tugged off the jeans. He twisted, knotted, folded, and twisted her jeans again to get every speck of water out. Then he slipped the pants on her legs and took her socks, performing the same functions.

Kathy turned to Jerry and examined his wound. The makeshift bandage had ridden up, exposing the red ragged crease across his back. The cold water had cleansed the wound and helped the bleeding to slow to nothing. She took what was left of her shirt and made a new dressing and secured the binding to hold it in place. While she was doing that, he cleared the gun and dismantled it, blowing water drops out of the chambers and reassembling it in a dryer state than before. He shook water out of the magazine, which didn't work effectively enough, so he took each bullet out and then shook the magazine. He had only four rounds left.

She still shivered but worked on Jerry. "I need your pants," she whispered. His well-defined legs were covered in a mass of bumps. Kathy noticed his muscles and ignored the chilled flesh.

She tried to twist the jeans, but his hands were stronger. They worked together and put everything back on. They hugged each other in gratitude for surviving the jump and getting out of sight. Jerry directed them up under the willows to a log washed against the bank. He pulled back the log and found sand underneath. They lay side-by-side and tried to restore warmth to their bodies. They both shivered. Kathy turned toward Jerry and said, "We need skin on skin if we are going to share body heat." She pulled up her jacket and did the same with him. They embraced. After a while the shivering began to subside.

Posse Commander Webber demanded clear and constant communication. He wanted to know where everyone was and what they were seeing. He didn't want to hear bad news. His excitement was unbounded when the call came in after the rifle report. The male soldier was down, the female would either stay with the body or be easily found. He directed his men to close on the location. Then he heard another gunshot. He wondered if that had been one intended for the female or a finishing shot on the male. He waited.

"Commander, Jackson's been hit! He took one in the chest. They're firing from behind some rocks. We need some help. We're pinned down, and Jackson needs to go to the hospital."

"I'll send help." The commander swore. His team was perfectly deployed to entrap and if the enemy was returning fire, they had to close carefully. He also needed to get his wounded out over rugged territory. The nearest were rushed to Jackson, and the rest were called in to converge on the scene of the shooting. All were cautioned. The final stage of the hunt was near.

When men reached Jackson, others were able to rush the rocks. They found markings on the ground and blood. Webber immediately sent teams on the trail. They couldn't be far. The rescue squad of four took turns carrying Jackson to the nearest road.

Webber's instructions were that it was an accident target prac-
ticing at one of their regular places. He turned to Bradley, "Do
your best. Find them!" Bradley took off at a trot, and Webber was
right behind.

He heard the exchange of fire later in the day, marveling at the
ability of the wounded soldier to keep going. He and Bradley ran.
They found one man watching where the two had been. "Where's
DeVries?" he asked.

"He is circling that way, and Cooper and Huxley are going
around the right." It wasn't a second before the walkie-talkie
crackled to life. The report was that they were not there. Webber
set his men in a wide flank, while he and Bradley followed
directly on the trail. He called the men further up the mountain
and ahead to close down. He wanted Bradley to slow down in
case the two might have gone to ground to fight it out to the last
bullet. He didn't want any more casualties. How could he explain
away several men with gunshot wounds?

The deer trail meandered around small trees and moderate-
sized stones. It was there that Bradley saw scuffmarks on the
path. He looked around and saw another mark further ahead.
He brushed the branch under the stone as he hurried along. The
stone rolled, attracting Webber's attention downward and causing him to stop. The log crashed down in front of him, injuring
his foot slightly. He jumped back in surprise. Hopping on one
foot, he contacted his men. "They're setting traps and snares…
watch out! They're not as injured as we thought."

Chasing slowed to a steady walk with every bush, tree, and
stone examined. Time seeped by. The ones closing from the front
moved faster. They didn't think the pair would be setting traps in
front of them. They did make the best use of cover and concealment as they approached the flat field of rock formations with
eroded lanes cutting through. It was open area, so they waited
and called. Webber told them he would be there soon. Minutes
later, they stared at each other across the open expanse. Webber

directed the teams to spread out and flush the soldiers out. They expected them to pop out somewhere in the rocks. The formations were scoured. They went to the edge overlooking the cliff and the alpine lake below. Bradley completely circled the field checking for signs of exit. The trail was blank. Webber sent teams around and down. He couldn't believe they would have jumped; it was too far to fall. Yet he knew them to be illusive and desperate. He waited, scanning in all directions with field glasses. Bradley was sent below to check for anything. He shook his head in disappointment. Webber watched.

Cooper and Huxley were working the bushes near the stream. One filled his water bottle and the other urinated into the bushes.

"We have to find them. If they get free, they'll talk and make more problems for our Colorado chapter."

"I know. The commander must be spittin' fire about now."

"He wants us ready for a quick nonviolent takeover next year. He doesn't want our area to be behind the other states."

"We'll just have to find them and end this. Damage control."

"Yeah, but how? They disappeared again."

"Well, they're soldiers. They're good at this."

"I hope Bradley can pick up their tracks. He's good at that kind of stuff. Not much else, but in tracking he's good. I wonder why Webber keeps him around. After losing the money, I thought for sure he'd get rid of him."

"You know the rumor don't you? Bradley may be his from Olivia."

"Olivia? You mean Ted's wife?"

"That's the rumor." They walked down stream on one side and back up the other side, looking for tracks. They looked for footprints or broken branches.

Bradley drew blank looks from the posse and a scowl from Webber. The Commander knew if they could be tracked, Bradley would be the one to do it. The only thing better was a bloodhound. Webber was forced to do what he had done the evening before, set out sentinels and watch till dark, then come out in the morning and search some more.

Their legs were still cold despite their being entwined together. Their torsos had a hint of warmth from mutual body heat. They clung to each other, willing their bodies to stop shivering. Kathy's jaw was clinched to keep it from chattering. It was hard to tell if they were more afraid of the cold or the posse. They whispered their agreement to stay in hiding until dark.

The shivering was momentarily interrupted by the sounds of voices and the rustling of grass. Their bodies froze. Two men were approaching, searching behind rocks, trees, and brush. They stopped next to the stream about three yards away. One peed into the willows. They could hear the liquid splash against the mud and sand. The voices were so close they could not miss a single syllable. Jerry lifted his head to scan the mud by the river. He could see indentations and marks where they had rolled out of the creek. He was sure this would be the end. He pulled out the pistol and aimed it up through the leafy branches in the direction of the voices.

They listened to the concerns of the speakers and then the story of Bradley's ancestry. They waited for the interrupted sentence with the pause while someone examined the disturbed soil, then the bushes being parted or maybe the hunters would fire rounds into the bushes to kill or flush them into the open. Their breathing stopped just like it did when they dropped into the lake. Minutes passed, and then they relaxed briefly as the men went downstream.

"I've got to do something about those marks." Jerry pointed to the muddy wash next to the water. The mud was still under the willows, but a careful tracker would make an effort to look under them. When the sounds of the men were gone, Jerry slipped out from behind the log and moved to the marks. He smoothed them over and patted them down. He reached into the stream and with his arm sloshed creek water up onto the mud erasing any signs. Then he backtracked, brushing the mud and sand higher up. The sand was deeper behind the log, so he scooped some up and cast it lightly over the entire area, dusting as he retreated. He got back to Kathy and worked at deepening the space behind the log. Digging with his hand and pushing with his feet warmed his muscles with the action. Soon there was an elongated foxhole for them to be completely hidden.

"We have about another half hour before sunset and maybe fifty minutes for twilight. Then they'll have difficulty tracking us," Kathy calculated in a hushed whisper.

"We'll move then," Jerry replied.

The scare helped them to forget the cold clothes they had on. They snuggled down in their pit and waited. Fifteen minutes later, Bradley came by scanning every square inch of the creek's edge. They could make out the white cowboy hat on his head through some of the leaves. They dropped down into the hole and held their breath. Bradley made a thorough check. He was losing light so he had to be quick and cover as much area as possible. He concluded they must have doubled back into the forest before they came into the rocks above the cliff. They relaxed as he moved away. Under the willows darkness came faster. No more sounds could be heard of men searching. They wanted to err on the side of being safe. They waited until all sunlight had faded above them.

"Let's try our luck," Jerry suggested. They rolled over the log and gently pushed aside the willow branches. Stepping on stones, they skirted the bush and stepped out in the night.

"Which way do we go?" Kathy asked.

"In the dark, it's better if we go down stream, eventually we'll hit a road," Jerry said. They hunched over almost to the point of using all fours. They wanted their forms to look like deer on infra-red sights. Jerry was thinking that it was near impossible for them to have a heat signature after the chill they had sustained.

The creek acted as an audio guide. They kept it to their left and followed game trails which were in abundance so close to water. At one point, they spooked an elk, and it ran over the hill never stopping. A doe and a fawn pranced away into the ferns and watched from a distance. True to Jerry's prediction, they hit a forest road heading down toward the east. It passed a reservoir fully enclosed in a chain-link fence. They walked carefully along the edge of a road and found a picnic site with log tables and permanent camp toilets. They took the opportunity to rest. Sitting on raised benches with a table in front of them was equivalent to a first class restaurant. Kathy laid her head on her arms and let the trials of the day slip out of her almost warm skin. She could easily go to sleep. Jerry kept vigilant listening for sounds on the road. "This posse is much bigger than just Colorado Springs or the state of Colorado. You heard what they said," Kathy started.

"It's disturbing to say the least. There's something huge scheduled for next year. No wonder there was an undercover agent spying on them. It's a takeover," Jerry commented.

"And…we know about it. We've got to get back and tell the authorities, whoever will listen."

"Problem is, who can we trust? The posse is everywhere," Jerry added.

"This is bigger than us. We have to get the word out even if it costs us our lives. Our oath as soldiers is to defend the nation against all enemies foreign and domestic. This is domestic!" Kathy was warming to the subject.

"I'm going to call Detective Soriano and see if he will listen," Jerry informed.

"If you bring up this conspiracy, he'll really think we're nuts."

"I'll try to get him the pictures I have on the other jump stick and when he believes us, then I'll tell him the rest. But I won't go in to see him until he's a true believer."

"Jerry, we might have killed someone today."

"I know. In self-defense."

"They were trying to kill us and this is the same as war. We have to protect ourselves. You did the right thing shooting him," Kathy put in her perspective.

"I'm glad you agree. From here on out we don't hesitate. They *have* to be exposed! We are the only ones who know." The days of fleeing and protecting themselves were taking their toll on his calm demeanor. His convictions were formed around a need to protect and generated from a feeling of not wanting to be a victim any more. Kathy brought him down.

"How does your back feel?"

"Better."

"When we get to some place safe, I'm going to clean out the wound and put a proper dressing on it. I don't want it to get infected."

"That's my Kathy." Jerry smiled. The sobriquet soothed Kathy all the way to her soul. It was a return gift she would cherish forever. It was the second indication he liked her in a special way. The first was under some ferns after she had declared her love. This was unprovoked and natural, worth a thousand hugs. The quiet evening sang with light breezes through the treetops. Kathy's heart sang louder.

Jerry could see he had hit a homerun. Kathy's face glowed like the reflection of a campfire. He felt pleasure in making her happy. It was a balm comforting his inner being. He thought of her words on the mountainside, *I don't want the man I adore to be alone in his heart.* No, he was not alone.

They stayed there soaking in the moment. Neither wanted to do the Hollywood embrace and rush beyond where they were at the moment. They had to get to town and find safety. Their relationship needed to grow more and Jerry had to say good-bye to his past with Sharon. Kathy needed to know that that aspect of his life was gone. It would require some time, which they felt was in short stock.

"I suppose we should try to get down to the Springs." Jerry rose from the table.

"Before we go, I'm going to use something that vaguely resembles a toilet," Kathy said flatly.

"And I'll do the same over here. I'll multitask," Jerry informed her.

"How is that multitasking?" Kathy was curious.

"I can watch for them at the same time." Jerry moved to the edge of the woods. A stiffer wind blew through the trees, blocking the sound of an approaching truck. When the wind subsided, Jerry could hear it clearly as it sped up the road.

"Kathy! Someone's coming! Hurry!" Jerry ran toward the toilet and then realized he would be in the headlights as the crew-cab pickup truck turned into the entrance. He ducked down and slipped back to the stand of pine. He could see the door of the commode open a crack in the full glare of the headlights. She was trapped. The door closed. The truck stopped, and a door slammed.

"I'll be quick," the husky voice echoed. As he neared the toilet, Jerry felt helpless and wondered what Kathy would do. The man grasped the door and found it locked from within. He hesitated, scanned the picnic area, and found no cars, campers, or even unauthorized tents pitched in the picnic area. He rattled the door stronger. Then he pounded on the door. It was apparent he felt something was amiss. He kicked the door, loosening the latch, and wrenched the door open.

Jerry was beside himself with worry. His thoughts ragging, he pulled out the revolver and held it at the ready. He watched the man come to full realization.

"Look what I found!" Three men piled out of the crew-cab. Kathy was yanked by the hair out onto the ground. The burly man pulled her over the ground, dragging her feet in the dirt. Her hands were up to her head, trying desperately to ease the pressure on her scalp.

"It's her! We got one."

"The other one must be close." Two of the men pulled out handguns, one held his to Kathy's head. "Come out or we'll kill her!" Kathy was on her knees. Another called on his cell phone.

"Commander, we got one. She was hiding in a toilet. Over here on Gold Camp road, near Bison Creek. At the picnic grounds. No, alone, but the other one should be close by." The conversation closed, and the individual snapped his phone shut. "The commander's coming our way."

"Jerry, run! Go tell the authorities! They're going to kill us anyway. You need to get away." She was yelling over her shoulder opposite from where Jerry was standing behind a tree. Her outburst yielded a yank and a kick from her holder.

"Gimme my gun. I'll put a bullet in her brain. That'll stop her yelling."

"Jerry, I mean it. Go! I love you!"

"Now isn't that sweet." He shook her head again. "Okay, Jerry, you've got to come out now, and we'll let her go."

Jerry saw Kathy reach into her pocket for the card knife. Now was the time for him to act. One man was distracted getting a gun out of the truck; another was looking into the forest opposite with his back turned, hand on his revolver. Jerry walked boldly out toward the five. Kathy saw him coming. She coiled up and drove the knife into the man's throat, twisted it like a bayonet, and retracted it. Her actions surprised one man, who gaped for an instant in her direction, the last moment of his life. Jerry shot him in the center of his chest while he tried to aim his pistol. He turned his gun on the other one who was looking the other way but was starting to turn, and plugged him in the back. The man at the truck had jumped at the sounds of gunfire, and Jerry was now close enough to risk a headshot, squeezing one off. He looked at Kathy, who was driving the point end of the knife into the chest of her attacker.

Hastily they kicked guns away from hands and checked for life. The man with the knife wounds was gurgling. Jerry looked at Kathy. They embraced.

"You're not very good at multitasking," Kathy spoke.

"I'm sorry, they came so fast."

"That's all right. I really wanted longer hair anyway," Kathy quipped.

"We need to get outta' here. Let's see what we can use." They picked up the revolvers. Jerry grabbed the cell phone of the one who had recently used it. It was an old, flip-style phone with no Internet access. Jerry kept it, They rummaged through the truck, finding long-range rifles with scopes and binoculars. Jerry was about to throw them in the bushes when Kathy spoke. "Let's drive the truck down the hill and ditch it. It'll put us farther away." They climbed in. Kathy took the wheel, turned the keys, and mashed the accelerator, spreading gravel over the bodies like when a dog scratches dirt over his poop. They raced down the hill.

Jerry took the opportunity to scrounge necessities: a rucksack, extra clips of ammunition, a first-aid kit, bananas, and water out of the back seat. Some of those he fished out of the truck bed by reaching through the back window. He packed them all in the pack. He wanted the 30-0-6 but wondered how he could carry it in the city. He then started to disassemble it, first the scope, then dropping screws and nuts in the pack. He separated the barrel from the stock. Everything fit inside, but the barrel poked out. He grabbed a camouflaged floppy hat and jammed it over the barrel. Then he tied it in place with a shoelace from a boot in the back seat. They were ready. Then he remembered the revolver he had used and realized his fingerprints were on it. It would implicate him even more in the eyes of Soriano. He remembered seeing some Armor All tire wipes in a plastic container in the back. He got them and wiped down the pistol repeatedly. Then he waited for the best time and hurled the weapon out the window and down a steep incline into a rockslide. It clattered between stones and out of sight. He then started cleaning everything he touched.

Kathy concentrated on her driving, slowing only for curves. As the lights of the city neared, she looked for a side road, found one, and drove up it until it turned into a trail. She crammed the hood into a bush and turned the motor off. Jerry took the keys, wiped them, and threw them into the weeds. Jerry made quick work of cleaning the steering wheel and the inside door panels. Then they walked down the road. A residential neighborhood near the five-star Broadmoor Hotel greeted them as they stayed to the dark sides of the streets. They worked their way away from the main road and into quiet avenues. The hike was minimal compared to the treks they made the last couple of days. Exhaustion dominated the fibers of their bodies. Visions of the deaths they had caused trespassed their thoughts.

"We had to be soldiers," Jerry read Kathy's mind.

"It's war. What else could we do?" Kathy sounded defeated.

"Kathy, it was them or us. We didn't have a choice. They're the bad guys."

"My scalp is reminding me of that fact."

"You did the right thing."

"So did you." Kathy walked to Jerry's side and put her head against his chest. He put his arm around her. They walked downhill in silence.

"Just do me a favor and remind me not to be in the kitchen with you when you're chopping carrots." His comment was an attempt to lighten the mood. Her inward response was to note his desire to be together in a house with her preparing dinner. It made her feel better.

⧉

At an upscale motel on HWY 115, which was South Nevada Ave, they decided to stay the night. Kathy left Jerry as he stood around the corner from the office. They needed to have a room on the first floor with a window in the back they could exit from if needed. The motel was not full, and she secured a room in the middle of the long building after taking five soggy twenties out of her pocket. She used the same story on the late-night clerk that she had used in Denver two nights before. Rest was their primary concern, however they wanted some of the clothes they had in storage. It was about three quarters of a mile away.

"You stay here, and I'll get our stuff," Jerry offered.

"No you won't. You're not going anywhere without me," Kathy retorted.

"There might be something open along the way. We can get something to eat. Ready?" They took the weapons and hid them under their jackets. Kathy's fleece had blood on it, and Jerry's had two bullet holes in the back, one entering, the other exiting. Checking for traffic and squad cars, they made it up to the Stor-N-Lock without being seen. They collected the large pack with clothes, other essentials, and several wads of bills. Jerry did not forget his computer and jump drives. They stopped at a midnight Taco Bell and a twenty-four-hour drugstore on the way back. In the room, they made ready for the next day.

"I think you should take a shower first," Kathy instructed.

"Do I stink that much?"

"No, I just want to scrub your back while you're in the shower. Keep your boxers on, though." She gave him a few minutes to knock the dirt off. Then she entered the bathroom, noting how his boxers clung to his body. She also noticed there was no ring around his neck. She looked for it and found it in the wastepaper basket. She rescued it and put it on the vanity. Opening the glass shower door, she gently scrubbed the wounds, adding a back rub as a loving extra. Exiting, she took the ring with her and then waited for him to come out so she could apply the dressings. She then showered, and they went to their respective beds.

Commander Webber drove into the parking lot to find four bodies scattered on the ground. He stopped his SUV at the entrance and got out. All were dead, one with an ugly wound to the neck. He was beside himself with frustration, more for the escape of the two than for the loss of life. He agonized over the situation these deaths put him in and what cover story he would have to manufacture to hide the manhunt he and these men were performing. He knelt by one and did not see his weapon. A quick check found the same for the others. His enemy must be armed with more guns.

Anger raged within. His original design to keep authorities from discovering the plans and preparation of the Colorado section of the posse, and thereby the nation, had spiraled out of control. These two soldiers were an enormous problem and repeatedly had proved they were difficult to defeat. He needed damage control. He clenched his fists, using them to pound on his legs.

Standing silently behind him, Bradley sympathized in his simple way. "They did it again." Webber wanted to scream at him, but his answer for how to cover this was there in the air. He found a way to implicate the soldiers with the deaths of his men. The bullets would be from the same gun with the same markings. He immediately called the men who had taken Jackson to the hospital.

"Norm, have you given anyone details about how Jackson got shot?"

"I told the nurses and doctors what happened, about the target practice and stuff."

"Any police officers?"

"No, but we expect them any minute. The hospital just phoned it in."

"Good, then just add one more detail. Say that you think you heard the sound of the gunshot off in the trees from behind the targets. That might make them think our two soldiers are still on the rampage. We want to blame the shooting on them. Make sure the doctor saves the bullet for forensics."

"Okay, sir."

Commander Webber returned to his four-by-four, put on gloves, and got out the tire iron, which had been lying next to Probasco. He took it and whacked the head of the man shot in the back. Then he dropped it about five feet away. It was an extra touch to prove it was the soldiers. He turned to Bradley and said, "Let's go." He drove down the hill.

CHAPTER 7

In the middle of the night, Kathy awoke sitting up with a start and a muffled scream. Her body was rigid and soaked in sweat. Her respirations were heavy heaves of fright.

"You can't sleep either," Jerry's voice came out of the darkness.

"I'm sorry, did I wake you?"

"No, I couldn't sleep. My mind keeps coming back to what happened today, I mean yesterday. I close my eyes and I see it. It makes me want to keep my eyes open. I can't shake it outta my head!"

"I'm reliving everything in my dreams. I'm so tired I need the sleep, but the nightmares…I'm so afraid of it all," Kathy panted with anxiety.

"I don't want you to be afraid." Jerry got out of bed and sat beside her. He put his arms around her, leaning his back against several pillows, holding her back against his chest. "Feel better?"

"With you, I always feel better," Kathy relaxed.

"Do you want to know what's going through my mind the most?"

"Yes," she indicated.

"You," he responded.

"Me?"

"I keep seeing that man pull you around by the hair. My jaw hurts from clinching my teeth every time I picture it. I didn't want you hurt, and I was frozen not knowing how to stop it.

Then I didn't care about me; I just walked at them planning on killing as many as I could, making sure my shots were accurate. I didn't want you to be hurt even in the smallest way. I wanted you to run to the authorities, not me. I wanted you to be the safe one, not me. You said you love me, and that makes me responsible for you." Kathy turned her head into his chest and nestled closer.

"Looking back at the scene, I realized that the reason I felt responsible was because I love you too. Love is a funny thing. You can love someone and not know it. Our attitudes and principles can cover it up. Now it's in the open, my mind has found it. It was there growing stronger all the time. I love you, my Kathy girl!" He kissed her on the head. She turned her face upward, and they kissed on the lips gently, lovingly, tearfully. With all the physical chaos and moments of dangerous fright they had lived through in the last couple of days, they only wanted the comfort of compassionate company and the settled feeling of belonging. Passion didn't own a place in this tender revelation. Their lives were beginning to weave into one.

They remained where they kissed, both sitting against the pillows. She had her hand on his shoulder half turned with her head on his chest; he caressed her hair. Sometime later he could feel her sleeping in his arms. He didn't leave her. He didn't want to. He relaxed and savored the feeling. No amount of exhaustion could induce him to sleep and lose this feeling. He would not move even if his body rebelled from sitting in the same position for hours.

Morning traffic noise broke into their consciousness. Jerry was still sitting up. Kathy was curled inside his arms. They disentangled themselves, intending to start regular wake-up activities. Kathy took two steps and bounced back to kiss Jerry on the lips. "Thank you for my restful sleep." Her actions added a pleasant surprise to his grogginess. He remembered why he was so sleepy. He slid down into the pillows and went to sleep.

A couple of hours later, he woke to the smell of breakfast with coffee, egg sandwiches, and hash brown nuggets. Kathy was in cut offs and a summer shirt, reading a piece of paper.

"Did you go out?"

"Yep, and I got us some breakfast. It's a little better than your pine needles."

"You went out alone?"

"Don't worry. I wore these"—she pointed to her floppy hat and sunglasses—"and I took my ripped jeans and made cut-offs." She stood to show off her creation, turning with one toe on the floor and the other foot flat. "Your knife is very helpful. I cleaned it and used it to cut the pant legs off. Come on. You must be hungry."

Jerry scratched his head, "What's that you're holding?"

"Our bill. It says, 'Mr. and Mrs. Ronald Stafford.'"

"You're good with making up names on the spot. I like it."

"I had to do something. I didn't want to use the same name as before." Jerry sat down at the little table. He noticed she had waited to eat with him. He could sense the subtle change that had come into their relationship. "Should we stay here another night?"

"I thought about that. If we keep going to different places, we risk being found. I paid for another night here, then we'll see," Kathy paused. "I took your ring out of the waste basket." She placed it on the table in front of his Egg McMufffin paper. He stopped chewing. "It might not have any value for you anymore, but you should trade it in for what its worth."

"You're right. Once it used to represent something, now it just means money. I'll turn it in when I get a chance."

"Jerry, it used to have good memories tied to it. You can't dismiss good times, they are a part of who you are, your history."

"Maybe later I can be more objective about the past."

"If you do, just remember I won't be jealous. The present and the future is what I want. Everything that has happened to you in the past makes you the nice person you are today."

Jerry thought about that and then said, "My clear thinking sweet Kathy."

They finished breakfast and refocused. Jerry came back to the list for the day. "I need to call Detective Soriano."

"Jerry, I think Detective Soriano is in danger too. If he stands up for us and goes after Webber, then he gets the full wrath of the posse on him."

"Then what we need to do is warn him and get these pictures to various agencies; like police departments and the FBI."

"And the news media," Kathy added. Jerry went into a thoughtful attitude. Kathy wondered what he was thinking. After a while she asked, "You seem to be in deep thought."

"Yes, I am. You're not going to like what I'm thinking. We are stuck in this problem. And we can't get out. The posse is supposedly everywhere. We have to do something big and expose these people. I want to catch them in the act somehow and call in the authorities. At the same time we have to send our proof to…well, everywhere."

They sat in quiet, reflecting for a few minutes, then Jerry began again. "We have to warn Soriano, but try to get him to believe us. Believe us enough not to send the police after us. We have our hands full with the posse, we don't need to get innocent officers in the way."

"What are you planning?"

"I think we need to fight back. I'm tired of being on the defensive. I want to be the hunters, not the hunted!"

"My sentiments exactly. Do you have a plan?"

"I'm beginning to build one. First we have to get some disguises and some transportation. We need to call Soriano."

The phone call came about 10 a.m. Detective Soriano was working on reports and committing smaller incidents to the stack of completed files. He looked at the folder he had dubbed the "Returning Soldiers" file. He answered the call from the desk.

Four bodies had been found in a picnic park up by Bison Creek. He grabbed his coat. When he got to the site, he found officers and technicians everywhere. Photographs were being taken. He would view them later. He wanted to take in the data first by himself, make assumptions, then see if the facts confirmed his assumptions. He saw the tire iron lying on the ground. It looked like a one-sided massacre, guns being the primary weapon with a knife and the iron bar. Three were shot, one stabbed to death. *What is the story?* he asked himself. *Where is their car? Why here at night?* The questions dominated his thinking. He would find the answers one by one.

He looked closer at the tire iron. It appeared to be off of a late-model car. They are usually smaller like this one, painted black and rarely used. This one appeared to have never been used. The lug nut socket still had original paint on the inside. He would see if fingerprints could be matched to any record. He got out of his crouch hovering over the tire iron and went to talk to the family who had discovered the bodies. He asked the same routine questions.

He got a call on his cell from the receptionist at the station.

"They called again?" he asked after opening pleasantries.

"Detective, they asked specifically for you. I told them you were out."

"Are they calling back?"

"Yes. I told them I would call you and you would call them back, but they didn't leave a number. Instead they said they'd call back. Caller ID indicates they are calling from a payphone."

"Give them my cell number when they call back. I want to talk to them." He hung up and tried to refocus on the situation at hand. He watched the lab technicians collect the evidence. Officers scoured the area nearby for any other evidence. Soriano went to a picnic table and sat on the table with his feet on the bench. His cell rang. It was from an unknown caller.

"Yes?"

"Detective Soriano, we have more jump sticks with the pictures of the murder on them. I've double-checked, and they're not blank. They're good copies," Jerry said.

"That should help your case immensely. Bring them in."

"We can't. We are being followed by the Patriot Posse, and they are trying to kill us. If we come in, the same thing might happen again like with Detective Probasco. You have to understand we are in danger."

"All right. Then can we meet?"

"Sir, I'm not sure that's the best for you."

"Why? Why wouldn't that be best for me?"

"You are in danger too. We don't want you to be hurt. The Patriot Posse is bigger than you think."

"That's nice, but I'm not buying it. Come in and we'll sort it out. You'll get a chance to prove yourselves," Soriano's voice was beginning to rise.

"Like I said, we can't."

"You're acting like fugitives."

"We *are* fugitives! But we're innocent. Everything we have done has been in self-defense. When I hit Detective Probasco in the head with the tire iron, it was in self-defense because he was shooting at us."

"You hit Probasco in the head?"

"Yes. It was either me hitting him or him shooting us. Our lives were at stake."

"You hit him in the head, in the car, and then wrecked his car with him in it?"

"He was not in the car. He was chasing us and shooting at us. I kicked out his taillight, but that's the only damage to the car."

"This is not adding up. Please come in."

"Sir, it would be better for you if you did not indicate that you are sympathetic with our situation. If you are and tell anyone that you think we are innocent, the posse might want to silence you."

"Now you are talking as if there's this big conspiracy. You have to understand I look at the basic facts and deal with the truth. You told me you hit Probasco with a tire iron. That means you have confessed to assaulting a police officer and putting him in the hospital! What am I supposed to do with that fact?"

"Sir, that is the truth and another truth is he shot at us almost putting us in a grave! What was I supposed to do?"

"Sgt. Svenson, I can assure you that I will be fair to the facts. Your talk sounds logical in many ways and in other ways it does not. The only proof you have is the pictures, and I don't have those. Bring them in and I'll look at them. Otherwise we are just going around in circles."

"Sir, Kathy wants to ask you a question. I'll put her on."

"Detective Soriano, you said you called our folks," Kathy started.

"That's correct."

"Then why did you send police officers out to my folk's house to get information?"

"I did not."

"Did the officers share their information with you after their visit?"

"No. No officers were sent."

"Then who sent them?"

"I do not know. I'll find out." Soriano did not like being on the defensive. He decided to turn the tables. "Sgt. Pelletier, where were you last night?"

"On the mountain running away from the posse."

"Were you at a picnic area near Bison Creek?" Kathy was silent for a moment. She knew she had to tell the truth. She also knew that this would implicate her and Jerry even more.

"Yes, sir, we were there."

"I'm there right now. Please tell me what happened." Kathy began by explaining briefly their flight off the mountain and her capture. She explained how she was trapped in the latrine. She emphasized, without embellishment, her abuse and the plan to "put a bullet in her brain" to keep her from yelling for Jerry to run and tell the authorities. Then she described the one-sided gun battle and her stabbing of her attacker in the throat. As she spoke, Detective Soriano could see the evidence of her words in front of him; the scuff marks where she had been dragged by her hair, the broken door to the bathroom and the knife wound in the neck. She detailed how they fled in haste to avoid Webber and explained how worried they were that he, Detective Soriano, would not believe them. She told them where to find the truck. He paused to get a policeman to locate the truck, telling him where to look. And then he cautioned her that they needed to come in under his personal protection.

"You can't do that. Because if word got out that you are protecting us, you will be their target. We need to protect you as much as you need to protect us." Her words were convincing. He wanted to believe, because almost everything she said was displayed in front of his eyes.

"Help me understand. Did you and Sgt. Svenson use anything else beside the revolver and the knife to kill these men?"

"Nothing else," Kathy answered.

"Nothing? Not even a tire iron?" Soriano probed.

"No, sir. Jerry used the tire iron on Probasco and left it there. We didn't have a tire iron at the picnic site."

"Where did you get the weapon?"

"We took it off Detective Probasco. It's his."

"I sense you are trying to tell the truth. In all the years I have been a detective, I've never had anyone be so forthcoming. I want to believe you, but—"

"Don't say it, sir, we're not coming in."

"Miss Pelletier, I have to tell you, I cannot call off the search for you without solid evidence. The police will still be under orders to take you into custody if they find you."

"We understand."

"Please call me again. You can use this number." He waited to see if she would stay on.

"Good-bye, sir."

Detective Soriano wanted the tire iron checked at the lab immediately. He knew what the results would be. He asked for fingerprints to be lifted from the bathroom, overriding arguments that there would be many prints from loads of people. He then drove to the sight of where Probasco's car was stored. He looked for a tire iron and found none. He saw the kicked-out taillight. Then he found a cut zip cuff in the very back of the trunk where they flew when the car hit the tree. He collected it for evidence. He called the police department in South Dakota, asking for the report of the visit to the Pelletiers'. There was no record of a visit or a report. He then went to the scene of the accident. He examined the tree that Probasco's car had smashed into. He reasoned that if an escape had happened, it most probably occurred at a stop sign. He went to the nearest and then slowly walked all over the vicinity. He found a trail and then a bullet casing. He carefully picked it up with a pen and put it in another evidence bag.

He made a quick visit to the hospital to snag a short conversation with his friend of many years. He knew he had to be extremely careful so as not to alert his friend that he was on to the truth.

"How are you doing?" Detective Soriano asked.

"Better," Probasco said.

"Good, I'm glad. What do the doctors say?"

"They say I can go home tomorrow. There's no bleeding in my brain. I'm hardheaded, I guess. Do you ever get claustrophobic? The CT machine is really close."

"I've never had to have a CT scan, so I wouldn't know." Soriano knew Probasco was trying to lead the conversation. "When will you be able to come back to work?"

"The doctors said I'm going to have to take it easy for a month or so. When they clear me, then I'll be back."

"Too bad, I could really use you now. I've got a quadruple homicide up at Bison Creek."

"Whoa, that's big. Got any leads?"

"No, not really. Not yet. We're checking for fingerprints. We haven't found the murder weapon yet, but we're still looking. Say, I have to get back to work on this murder. Is there anything I can do for you? You know, like safeguard your service revolver. Did your wife take it for you?" Soriano watched Probasco's eyes widen, look to the left, and down to the floor.

"I don't know where it is—in the car, maybe. Ah, can you check for me?"

"Sure."

"Thanks."

"Get better okay? Gotta go." Detective Soriano left the room. He checked the time and planned on accessing Probasco's cell records from that moment forward.

"I think Detective Soriano believes us now. Maybe not completely, but he's sympathetic," Kathy informed.

"I hope he takes our warning."

"Now what?" Kathy asked.

"We look for a car." The pair left the second pay phone that they had used that morning and went immediately to a line of stores in a strip mall. They shopped for necessities.

In their new disguise they looked more like long-haired easygoing college students. They had found a wig shop, and Kathy got a strawberry blonde wig and coaxed Jerry into a shorter black-hair version. They bought flip-flops and old green army field jackets. She still had the cut-off jeans on, but he had switched to some green khakis. Kathy took some brown eyebrow pencil to Jerry's blond brows. At a distance it would do, but kissing close it wouldn't work. They walked holding hands.

An older neighborhood is where they looked first. They sauntered up and down streets looking for cars with "For Sale" signs in the windows. Most of the afternoon was spent searching. They tried a trailer park and then another better residential area. The cars they had seen previously did not look like they could travel two blocks. The ones in the slightly high rent district were too expensive. They went to a college campus and struck it rich. There were several cars for sale, including a pickup in need of a good paint job. It had a price and a phone number in the window. They went to the nearest dormitory and used the pay phone. The owner was living one building over and consented to come down right away.

They checked out the little truck. It purred when the engine was turned on. The owner proudly explained he had worked on it himself. The reason he needed to sell was to pay for tuition. He was desperate for money and really didn't want to part with the truck. They met his asking price without trying to wicker a better deal. He went and got the deed and the registration and signed the back, effectively handing it over to them when they handed him the cash. They explained they were headed to Seattle to school there and needed transportation. With the deal done, he got a screwdriver out of his pocket ready to detach the license plates. Jerry asked if he could let them use them as they didn't want to get a new car permit here in Colorado and do it again in Washington. When he hesitated, Jerry offered him two hundred dollars. It was enough persuasion.

"What's next?" Kathy asked as they drove up Academy Blvd.

"What's next is some supplies, and after that some offensive equipment to turn the tide in our favor."

"Are you going to tell me your plan?"

"Yes, of course. I will need you to help me carry out my plan."

Webber didn't know what to do, and patience was the least of his virtues. He sent his men crisscrossing the streets of Colorado Springs, searching for anyone on the streets who resembled the two soldiers. He sat at his desk, planning his search and his image in the department. The everyday issues of leadership in the department kept him busy. His concerns were for finding and snuffing out the two who could ruin his life. If he called Soriano to talk, he might give the impression that he knew he had been implicated and was fishing for information. He wanted Soriano to think all was well. The fact that the two were on the run was in his favor. If they disappeared altogether, then their statement would appear to be mere fabrications. He had to maintain a business-as-usual exterior.

Shift report was the moment he could look his best. He gave out shift responsibilities and reminded the officers of new news and ongoing cases. He was somewhat pleased that Soriano had found time to attend and was against the wall in the back of the room. He mildly slipped in the unfinished issues of the two suspected car thieves believed to be soldiers and never mentioned that they had been in the station and signed statements. He exuded a persona of a leader handing out routine, humdrum, everyday actives of a municipal police force. He asked Soriano if he had anything to add.

Soriano gave a description of the quadruple homicide, adding the little that was common knowledge and explaining the concern that lab results might yield some leads. Officers were to be on the lookout for suspicious activity and to be open to tips from concerned citizens that might break this case. He added that the news media was asking for information. He ended with, "That's all we have for now."

Webber excused the shift and exited to his office to visibly shuffle papers and read reports. Soriano watched Webber with a placid exterior. He took a few notes during the initial briefing and read from his notebook when he spoke. The two leaders were slow dancing around normalcy.

It was proper for Soriano to update the Lieutenant about the two soldiers. He knocked on the doorjamb of his open office door. "Ed, I need to update you on the latest about the two fugitives. You were off the last couple of days."

"Go ahead." Webber kept his head down, shuffling papers.

"The two soldiers came in on their own to give a statement. Their story about the stolen car holds together in many ways, but they have some rather exaggerated accusations. I think they may be suffering from PTSD or Afghanistan flashbacks. They seemed real nice and very afraid. I wanted to do a psychevaluation on them and do another interview when they had time to cool down or after some medication. They made statements that show they are collecting data from the environment and reassembling it into wild stories. For example: They saw you and me on TV and they have taken your name and put it into a fabricated story about a murder they witnessed." Webber stopped shuffling and looked up. "They said they have pictures to prove it and gave me a jump stick supposedly with everything on it. The jump stick was blank. I wanted to gain their confidence and put them up in protective custody at a hotel. They thought it was for their protection, but really it was to keep an eye on them. They bolted. Probasco dropped them off at a restaurant, and they ran. Now we're trying to find them again. My best guess is that the flashbacks are affecting them again. They must be hiding somewhere in fear."

"Okay, thanks for the update. So, I'm wrapped up in this dream of theirs? What do you make of that?"

"I'm no psychologist, but the statements they made are worthless because they ran," Soriano explained.

"When you find them or if they come in again, lock 'em up. Put them on a seventy-two-hour mental health hold. Who knows what their minds are going to tell them to do next? Then we'll let the shrinks make heads or tails of their stories."

"Roger that. That's all I've got."

"Soriano, keep me informed." Webber's head went down to read and shuffle more papers.

Jerry's mind was in fourth gear. His thoughts traveled at highway speed. Ideas, places, and strategies were flowing into a solid design. Kathy was adding ideas and refining his scheme. They focused on the fight and not the retreat. They were going to get the job done first and work the aftermath later. They both knew that all the rest of their lives would be tainted with this experience. And they had to finish what they knew to be true in the here and now. They were two soldiers riding into battle.

They went to a grocery store to get supplies, food, and water. They bought more clothes, which would help them alter disguises. They purchased mailing supplies and a printer to hook up to Jerry's laptop. They acquired a portable CD player with recording capabilities and extra batteries. They went to an army surplus store and got some familiar and comfortable sets of army camouflage uniforms, which have infra-red blocking capabilities. They purchased sleep systems with foam mats to which they were completely accustomed. Their plan obsessed their thoughts. They had very little time and wanted to work as fast as possible to avoid discovery. Their greatest danger of being found was when Jerry entered a gun and ammo shop. He used night to cloak his approach. Kathy was on over-watch outside. He needed extra bullets for the various guns they had in their plan. However, he needed something more. Kathy knew what he was after, and had asked him how he knew this particular store had what he needed. He told of how he was out with Chuck Staley one evening, and Chuck evidently wanted to show off and brought him to the same shop. He watched as Chuck gave the passwords and the man behind the counter took them to a back room where a false wall was removed and a stash of illegal weaponry was in a storage room. This room was reserved for "special" citizens.

When Jerry approached the counter, he worried that the passwords might have changed. The individual behind the counter was the same as the night he had accompanied Chuck.

"Can I help you?"

"Yes, I was here last year with my friend, and I need a few things. First I need some ammo in these calibers." Jerry handed him a detailed list. "One box each should do." The clerk pulled the boxes of cartridges off the large floor-to-ceiling shelf and piled them on the counter. Jerry paid for them and then waited.

"Would you be needing anything else?" That's when Jerry spoke the passwords. There was a nervous interval for Jerry as the man paused, looked around the shop, and then motioned for him to follow. Just like the year before, he was taken to the room. He asked for four grenades. He was handed a thick brown heavy cardboard box containing four lethal spheres. The black numbers were printed on the box on two sides followed by "4-each" at the end of the line of numbers. When he opened the lid, he found smooth round green grenades looking exactly like the ones he had qualified on in basic training. "Anything else?"

Jerry answered with, "Yes, do you have any night scopes?" He was shown two types, and he picked out the best. He paid with a bundle of cash and placed the box of grenades with the night vision devices in his pack and left. He found himself needing to breathe when he got to the truck, which was parked at the less visible side of the building. He now had the necessary weapons to accomplish his mission. Kathy joined him a second later.

"I'm guessing everything went without a hitch?"

"I'll say yes when we're safely away from here."

They drove out of the parking lot, taking a couple of quick unnecessary turns onto side roads. Kathy watched the windows and doors of the shop as they left to see if anyone was watching them or reading the license plate. Then she looked back to see if anyone was following. She couldn't see anyone.

"So, you walked in, said the password, and they sold you the grenades no questions asked?"

"That's about it. I guess it pays to have friends in low places. From what I remember from last year it looks like their inventory is down. They must be selling more stuff."

"To the posse, I bet. They're stocking up for next year," Kathy retorted.

"Or for us," Jerry answered.

⸭⸭⸭

They stowed most of their purchases in storage, being careful to not expose themselves to security cameras or park the truck where the plates could be read. Back at the motel room, they began working on writing their experience in detail. They assembled mailing packages and labeled them for the FBI, both local and national offices; for the police departments of Colorado Springs, Denver, and major cities on the west and east coasts; for the *Colorado Springs Gazette* plus national newspapers; one each for their parents; and finally they addressed one to Detective Soriano. They were careful not to mention him by name in the narrative, as they didn't want him to be the target of the local posse. They left the packages unsealed so they could add any final notes after the mission was complete.

It was very late when they were done. They felt good finishing the job and putting everything in a large box labeled and addressed to "Detective Soriano." They reasoned that if they were unsuccessful in defeating the local posse, eventually someone would open the storage compartment, find the box of packages, and notify him. One complete set was tucked away in a backpack. With their plan for informing the authorities now complete, they could focus on other steps in the effort to stop the Patriot Posse. The next couple of days would be filled with excessive work. Tired, they stretched out on the bed and talked. Jerry had his hands behind his head. Kathy lay with her head on Jerry's chest.

"I've got two possible plans for the money," Jerry said.

"What do you have in mind?"

"I think we could use it to defeat the posse by mounting a campaign of exposure, or…we can use the money to help charity."

"Why not both?" Kathy asked. "These reports we are sending out might do the trick. We could keep some money in reserve just in case they don't work as well as we planned in mounting a campaign of exposure. We could use the rest to help the Afghani children or some other agency."

"We could invest it in some safe securities and make it possible to keep on giving in the future," Jerry thought out loud.

"Yes, that would make it possible for us to spread it around to other causes or be ready to fight the posse if it should raise its ugly head again," Kathy postulated.

"We just have to survive the next couple of days, first," Jerry reminded. The thought sobered the two, and they remained quiet. It took only a moment to fall asleep with the lights still shining on their tired forms.

CHAPTER 8

Morning sun streaming around the curtains made the room lights insignificant. They bolted out of bed, because they knew they had mountains of work to accomplish. They dressed in jeans and sweats. There was a pause in the bustle that caused them to cease their activity and look at each other. Kathy came to Jerry, wrapping him in an embrace.

"Have I told you today that I love you?"

"No, but I know it anyway." Jerry kissed her ready lips. "I love you."

"That makes five nights we've slept together in the same bed without having made love and one night in the same room. That has to be a record for two people who have professed love for each other," Kathy said in wonder.

"What can I say? I'm an old-fashioned guy."

"You're not tempted?"

"I would say that some of those nights didn't count with the circumstances and the cold, and the fact that I didn't know you loved me and I loved you. Besides we have been near total exhaustion."

"You're not attracted to me sexually?"

'Yes, I am, but…" Jerry blushed.

"But what?"

"You know…I…" Jerry paused.

"You can't?" Kathy sounded as gentle as a flower.

"I won't."

"What does 'won't' mean?" she inquired.

"It means I never have…by choice," he said pointedly. Kathy was bewildered. Her mind was putting together the meaning of a man in his twenties who hadn't had sex. It was not something one hears about in this world. She was embarrassed, pleased, proud, and gratified. She couldn't say anything. She didn't know what to say. Her mind went to Sharon. *Sharon didn't deserve this man! I don't deserve this man!* Yet, she counted herself lucky to have heard him say he loved her. Her arms strengthened in their embrace.

"Jerry, I respect you so much!" She hoped he would not ask her if she had planned to wait until she was married.

"Thanks, my Kathy girl." Jerry gave her another long kiss. Kathy was gratified that she didn't have to talk anymore on the issue. She changed the subject.

"So what's first?"

"We have to load supplies. We have to make recordings on the CD; some from the script I wrote last night and others just noises. Then we have to deliver everything and cache it at the mineshaft. And—"

"Are you sure the old mine will do the trick?" Kathy cut in.

"Pretty sure. I took a lot of pictures of it last year. I've been in it exploring. Oh, and I forgot to mention we need to make false IDs."

"False IDs?"

"Yes, that's a big discussion we need to have. It has to do with how we are going to get away. It's part of our exit plan." Jerry looked concerned, because of Kathy's possible reaction.

"Is that something we need to do now? We have a lot to do, to set up, and we need to practice."

"I suppose it can wait for now. Are you ready to read the script together?"

"Yes, let's get that done right away." The pair put their heads together to read Jerry's script. They didn't put any emphasis in it as yet; they familiarized themselves with the words and changed some cumbersome sentences. They needed Kathy to laugh and giggle, which she did poorly on the spur of the moment. Jerry wasn't worried. They timed it at about thirty minutes of sound. And Jerry said that it would be enough because he would repeat it on several tracks and the CD would play it over and over. They settled down to the final rehearsal with emotion and then the taping.

They recorded the words and paused for Kathy's laughter and giggles. She was not too sure. Jerry turned on the recording and proceeded to tickle her. He went for her sides and up under her arms. It totally surprised her, and she forgot the recording. She hid her ribs with her arms and said, "Don't! Don't you dare! I'm warning you!" The tickling continued all over the bed. She stifled a laugh and in place of that had a low-level giggle that morphed into a scream and then an outright laugh. She let loose the laughter when Jerry kissed and tickled at the same time. She turned the tables and started to assault his ribs. He let his joy release and laughed with her. It was everything they needed for the recording and more. They were on the bed facing each other, Kathy sitting on top. It was sobering for both to realize they were turned on. She felt embarrassed. *Have I gone too far?* she wondered.

"I'm sorry. I didn't mean to get carried away," Kathy apologized and climbed off of him and sat on the bed looking away.

"Don't be sorry. I started it." He looked at Kathy with worry. "Are you okay?"

"I'm all right, just worried. We've got a lot to do." Kathy straightened her shirt and stood.

Jerry could tell there was a change in her usual upbeat demeanor. He guessed. "I know we are going to be doing some dangerous stuff. I don't want you to be worried about me or us or you. We'll be okay. We've planned this out, and there are safeguards. We'll be all right. Can I count on you not to worry about us?"

"I promise I won't be worried about what we have to do." Kathy wasn't sure how they should talk about her real worry. She didn't want to lose him. She wanted to think about her situation and figure out a way to tell him…or not tell him. She plunked the long blonde wig on her head and then the floppy hat and sunglasses. "I suppose we should get going."

With that, Jerry loaded and stacked their backpacks and equipment they had in the room. The truck was perfect for hauling. They dumped all of it in the truck, returned the keys to the office, and drove to Stor-N-lock. There they added what they needed and left what they would keep safe. Piled on top of everything in the locker was the box of packages. A note indicated that Detective Soriano should be contacted about the contents of the box. They steered the truck south of town and onto HWY 115 toward Cañon City. It was an hour drive to Forest Road 67 where they would turn back north toward the mining town of Cripple Creek. They had a chance to talk.

"So you think we need false IDs?" Kathy started without preamble.

"Here's the way I figure it. If we are successful with the local posse, we'll still be the objects of hate from any other members of the posse wherever they exist. That means anywhere in the United States. We have to change our identities and live under those new identities somewhere away from here and away from South Dakota, don't you think?"

"You've been thinking about the future. You're suggesting not just false IDs to use as we need them, but actually changing who we are."

"Yes, what has happened to us is they have stolen our lives. We can no longer be who we were," Jerry said flatly.

"That's sad." Kathy was thoughtful.

"It is sad. I agree. I was thinking, necessary, if we want to live."

"But, Jerry, that means we could not use our bank accounts and the college credits you and I have earned. Our financial credit records would all be gone. The deposit I got for my car I traded in before our deployment, for a new one when I got back from Afghanistan, can't be used. I would have to start from scratch." Kathy totaled the facts. "And, another thing we would have to end our work as reservists for the army. We would lose our time served."

"The fact is we have no other choice. How can we ever be sure the posse or even the remnants of the posse will give up on us and let us lead normal lives?"

"We have to be someone they don't know," Kathy said dismally. She went into deep thought, alternating her thinking between the adjustments it would take with futile stabs at ways they could return to pre status quo. She couldn't come up with anything. "I guess we'll have to do it."

"That's my Kathy," Jerry encouraged. His encouragement drove a spike into her heart. She thought, *Will I still be his Kathy when he finds out I am not like him?* Her breath was heavy. And the only way to shake off the dreaded thoughts was to go back to Jerry's line of thinking.

"If I can't use all the money I saved during our mobilization because we are changing identities, then I want to use it now."

"What did you have in mind?" Jerry asked inquisitively.

"I'm going to buy my folks a specialty van with a ramp for my dad's wheelchair."

"How are you going to do that?"

"Watch me. Can we stop at Cañon City before we go on?"

"Okay. I hadn't thought of my bank account. I should do something too." The pair drove into town and found public phones close enough to see each other across the street. Kathy made four calls; one to a brother to get the number to the one car dealer in her home town, one to her bank manager, then to the dealership, and then her parents. It took almost forty-five minutes. Jerry made four calls, and it took less than thirty minutes to finish. One call was to his folks to explain away his extended delay in getting back to his hometown. He bought two lattes at the nearest café and joined Kathy on her side of the street. Her phone conversations took longer. They went into a small Mexican restaurant for lunch.

"My mother was not very happy when I said I was not coming home for a while."

"Did you tell her you were changing identity?"

"No. I just said I needed to work on these false accusations and clear my record. She got a little weepy. Then I told her I called Harry Halstrum at the dealership and arranged to buy a van with a ramp for dad. She cried. She wants me to come home."

"I can see where she's coming from. She loves you, and she wants her perfectly wonderful daughter to be near her," Jerry complimented. Kathy didn't feel so perfect.

"So what did you do?" Kathy shifted topics.

"I called the Afghan Children's Relief Fund and made a sizable donation on my debit card. I left about a thousand in my account for another idea I have."

"Jerry, that's a lot of money. Will your bank allow that kind of a transfer?"

"I called my bank, gave my phone password, and pre-cleared it."

"I kinda did the same thing, only in my small town everybody knows everybody else, so they knew me when I called. When I get home, I'll have to sign some documents. Harry totaled up the bill with my trade-in from before the deployment and my account that had money from my army savings, which was supposed to be my trousseau. It looks like I'll have somewhere near seven hundred left over. So why did you keep a thousand in your account?"

"I can use it to lay a false trail when we exit this mission."

"Did the raccoon have a bank account too?"

"What?"

"You know, the raccoon in the story *Where the Red Fern Grows*, the one who taught you how to disguise your trail?" Kathy smirked.

"Yeah, that raccoon. Pretty smart animal, huh? Ah, my Kathy, we are going to need to use the posse's money to start new lives."

"As far as I'm concerned, it's not their money anymore. They don't deserve it," Kathy said flatly.

"Well, it's set then. We'll put the posse behind bars, so to speak, change our identities, and then get out of Dodge City before the sun goes down."

"You make this sound like an upside down western where, instead of the good guys getting falsely accused and almost hung, the bad guys get put in jail for the right reasons, and then they live unhappily ever after."

"Yeah you're right, this is all very upside down. The good guys, the police, are chasing the good guys, us, who are chasing the bad guys, the posse, who are chasing the good guys. No one seems to be running away...not yet anyway."

After lunch they drove back to Forest Road 67 and up Phantom Canyon. Jerry didn't have any trouble locating the one old gold mine out of the hundreds that dotted the hillsides. From his meanderings of before and the many pictures he had taken, he knew this country by heart. They parked the truck partly concealed in some brush and carried their armory up the hill and stashed it away secretly. Then they started unloading the supplies. They were heavier, and it took a lot of lugging to move water bottles and canned foods up to the mine. They found the mine almost the same as it was a year ago. Jerry noticed that some agency had boarded up the entrance better than before and added signs of restriction barring the curious from entering the area. He needed a crowbar to open up the entrance again. He broke boards and laid them to one side for use later.

They returned to the truck to get the camping supplies. They placed all the items in concealed locations and returned for the truck. They drove back down Phantom Canyon Road and then back up the next canyon, Golden Park Valley, to the southwest. When they were roughly adjacent to the gold mine, they found a quiet ravine with numerous pine trees and serviceberry bushes able to conceal the truck from view. They left the keys under a rock in the truck bed and began the hike over the ridge near Mitre Peak. They had enough time to set up their observation points and find a suitable place nearby to layout the sleeping bags and created an austere center of operations.

Jerry then made his first call using the cell phone off of one of the attackers at Bison Creek.

"Hello. Who is this?"

"This is Mr. Svenson. I think you have been looking for me."

"How did you get my private number?"

"One of your goons from the Patriot Posse called you just before we took them out."

"Why are you calling me?"

"We want more money," Jerry demanded.

"That's absurd. You have enough money."

"I hardly think a couple of hundred thousand in cash is enough to live on and stay away from a posse that is nationwide."

"You can cash the bonds."

"Now it's my turn to say that's absurd. You and I both know we would have to have an agent to sell them, and when we returned to pick up the money the police would pick us up." He lied. Jerry winked at Kathy.

"How much money do you want?"

"One million in cash, unmarked bills with no dye bombs—"

"I don't have that kind of money. I won't pay you anything."

"Oh, you will. You see I have video of you killing that under-cover agent, and all I have to do is turn it in. I will exchange that video, both copies plus the original SD chip from the camera, for the assurance that you will leave us alone forever." Jerry knew there were holes in his blackmail scheme and had put them there purposely to lure Webber. "Oh, and don't tell me you don't have the money because you can take it out of your Patriot Posse slush fund."

"Where are you? I can bring you the money tonight."

"You said that too fast. I know you would have to cash out a lot of money from whatever bank account you are using for your secret society of killers. That would take some time. I'm a nice guy. I'm going to give you the time you need. I'll call you back either tomorrow night or the next night to tell you where and when. Good-bye."

Kathy had listened carefully to the conversation on speaker-phone. "So you think he's going to track us down?"

"I'm counting on it. He'll get the phone record and find which tower this conversation was relayed from. He'll know we called from somewhere near Cripple Creek. Tomorrow I'll call him again to tell him where to drop the money. That will help him get a better triangulation on our location. Now the waiting begins."

They changed into their newly acquired army uniforms and started setting up a routine for observing the area. They ate and planned the final preparations.

CHAPTER 9

Commander Webber informed his followers. He immediately started to track down the phone records with the cell phone company and discovered the Cripple Creek location. He laid plans to capture the two by placing a few men around the town, watching for possible matches to size and age, just in case the couple was staying in the area. He gave orders for them to watch and inform. He had to get them quietly out of town, finish them off, and, if possible, find the whereabouts of the money...then hide their bodies. He needed most of his team when the time came. He knew them to be elusive and deadly, and he couldn't make a mistake and lose men again.

He did not want the police involved; it had to be a posse operation. He had Bradley ready to search for tracks if they were found to be outside of town. He planned his answers to the phone call.

Bird song woke Jerry and Kathy before dawn. They had a cold breakfast and started sorting objects into the areas of need. They knew the hostile sides would be locking horns. They explored the mine with flashlights and found the perfect place to lay their trap. They set the CD player in an alcove of rock out of sight from the main bore into the depths. It was on the other side of a downward shaft that they laid planks across with ropes attached on the far side away from the entrance to the mine. They strung trip wires at ankle level and fastened them to bells as an early warning system. They then returned to the surface to dig shallow graves under a large sheet of rusted corrugated metal. The metal covered the graves, and with the exhumed dirt carefully carried away, they could detect no disturbance around the metal cover to tip off the approaching foe. The grenades were left in the box hidden behind some support beams near the entrance and ready for the moment they were needed. Old wire and debris were kicked to the side of the tunnel to make clear the entrance path. To one side of the rail bed leading deep into the mine was a drainage ditch set lower than the path. Jerry cleared that drain as it exited the mine. At the entrance he placed a heavy beam and dropped the broken boards from the door randomly leaning over the heavy beam.

Lastly, they placed their lookout stations. They built them up with protective logs and rocks and then placed in one prominent position the thirty-ought-six with scope and extra ammunition on a built up support of dirt with an excellent field of fire. At the other position they placed extra ammunition and a revolver. In both places they left sticks of gum and some finishing nails. They had complete over-watch of the valley up to the opening of the canyon miles away from Cripple Creek and over the ridge to their rear looking to the east and descending to the plains. The highest observation point would be their primary position for night and day.

They hiked up the ridge to the west opposite the old gold mine. At the top they were able to get a good signal on the pilfered cell, and called Webber.

"I'm not ready yet," Webber answered the call without the normal hello.

"I didn't think you would be. I called to tell you I want the money in large bills in two rucksacks, no tricks." Kathy had to stifle a giggle at Jerry's usage of movie lingo. Jerry smiled back at her. "I'll bring the money when I get it. Where do you want me to come?"

"I'll call you later to see if you have it. Then I'll decide." He hung up without courtesy.

The two grinned at each other. From here on out they needed to be sharp. Webber's men had to be closing in reasonably soon. They planned their next call from up the valley more to the east. Perhaps the cell would pick up a signal from the town of Penrose to the southeast.

✺✺✺

At sunset they sat at the top of the ridge watching. They ate chili-con-carne cold out of cans. Occasionally they would take up the field glasses and scan the hills for movement. They could see deer cautiously ambling toward sources of water. One vixen with a long bushy red tail led her kits to optimum places to hunt for mice. Birds sang night songs. It was time for peace, but not for the two.

"I have to make the call, and I need to go over there." Jerry pointed to the east. "Watch my back with the NVGs."

"I will. Please be careful," Kathy urged. They both scanned the area he needed to travel. Silently he slunk into the bush. She watched his back, top to bottom. She had to remind herself she needed to search for other movement besides his. As darkness closed, she switched to the night-vision devices that soldiers call NVGs. No movement was detected that was in human, two-legged form. Lots of other warm bodies were out there. Half an hour later, Jerry reached a top where he could see the lights of Penrose below and the glow of lights from the city of Pueblo almost to the horizon. He turned on the phone to see that a phone call had been attempted. The number matched Webber's. He called anyway.

"I see you tried to contact me."

"I'm not ready with the money. I need another day," Webber demanded.

"You're a talented man. I thought you could get it faster than that. You disappoint me."

"Getting the money in the form of a cashier's check is easy. Getting cash is more difficult. I need more time."

"I'll give you one more day. I don't want to have to send off the video unnecessarily because you can't do a simple little task. You don't want me to think you're really dumb now, do you? I'll call tomorrow." Jerry left the ridge and started back.

Kathy could see him as a fluttering flock of movement as he moved through trees and disappeared behind hillocks. His army uniform scattered his heat signature when viewed through the scopes. Knowing his purpose she could piece together his actions. He looked like a phantasm. She scoped the hillsides in thought and wishful thinking, not paying attention to what she was looking at. She kept coming back to Jerry's fuzzy form as it marched through the trees. She saw him stop and use his scope to check the area in front of him and then look at her in her hidden position. She wanted to wave but knew it was not smart. He was almost there when she saw two individuals edge along the ridge to their north. She was higher and looking down upon their glowing forms as they were portrayed in the scope. She switched from them to Jerry and could tell that they might be able to see his aura when he was near to her position if they had the same night seeing equipment. She waited for him to stop and look at her. She signaled that he should stop and approach low. She went back to watching as they climbed higher. She tried to pick out their forms and decipher whether they were armed. No game hunters should be about this early in the summer and definitely not at night. Jerry approached low and quietly. He almost startled Kathy.

"What do you see?" he whispered.

"Two coming up the ridge there."

Jerry put his scope on them. It was while he watched that they chose a place to stop. They settled into a blind behind some logs. They wrapped themselves in blankets and watched out to the northwest. The pair could see they were using low light illumination devices too. Their backs were to the hill, and they were below the crest of the ridge so as not to silhouette themselves to the sky. They were three-quarters of a mile away.

"I'm going to sneak up on them and listen to the conversation," Jerry informed Kathy quietly.

"Jerry please don't, it's too risky," she pleaded.

"I'll be careful. I'll stay behind the ridge out of sight. Don't worry. I just might be able to get some intel. Besides, I've got James Bond with me," he whispered back while patting his revolver.

Jerry slipped over the ridge with the silenced PPK and ran out of sight down the opposite side until he was near their position and then crept the rest of the way. He came out just above them and only had to adjust ten yards to one side to hear them. One was on the phone, finishing a conversation.

"...Yes, sir, Commander, understood. We'll observe, and when we see something we'll report it. We are not to engage until everyone is in place.... Yes, we're okay. We have enough food, and we had a big meal before coming out here.... Thank you, sir... will do."

Jerry listened and felt he had struck it rich. This was more than he hoped for. He had observers in a great place who when they were seen, they would call in the rest of the posse. The trap was set. Before he left, he circled down and aimed his scope across the men to see their angle of sight. They could not see the entrance to the mine from there, only the top of the shack built in front.

Bradley was eager to prove himself. He sat in Webber's kitchen, waiting for the word to go out after the soldiers. Webber, however, didn't want him to screw this up. He would use him for tracking, but watching was obviously not his best suit. He wanted him under his thumb. Bradley listened to the one-sided conversation as his commander directed the men under his control.

"They're somewhere near Cripple Creek. The cell signal bounced first off of a Cripple Creek repeater, then off of a Cañon City repeater. The last one, a few minutes ago came off of a Penrose repeater. They are moving around in an area southeast of Cripple Creek… Tomorrow… Yes, I have Gary and Ted in an area where they can watch any activity… What I need you to do is be there tomorrow morning before sun up… Thanks."

The phone rang. Webber felt the vibration first and heard the first ring before he answered. He got an idea he would try after he finished this call. "George, thanks for calling back. I need you tomorrow, early at Cripple Creek…south side on sixty-seven… four a.m. Good, thanks. Out." Webber called his sentinels back.

"Gary, I'm going to call the soldiers back right now. If their phone is on, you might be able to hear it. Listen carefully. Okay… out." The commander redialed Jerry and got his dead posse member's voice mail. It must have been switched off. He called Gary back just in case. They hadn't heard anything.

"Bradley, I want you to meet me here at my place at three a.m. Be ready. Now get some sleep. I'm going to need you."

"Okay, sir." Bradley left.

Jerry sneaked back to Kathy and informed her of how ideal the situation was with the two sentinels below them, and they then watched for a while together. They scanned all sides for more indications of watchers.

"I kinda insulted Webber a little when I talked to him. Tried to make him angry. He called me when I had the phone off. He said he needs more time to get the money in cash, and that's why he called. I gave him one more day."

"It looks like he has a pretty good idea where we are because of those guys."

"Yeah, what I heard from them was the tail end of a conversation about them not doing anything until everyone is in place. They're just supposed to observe. I'm sure they were talking to Webber."

"That sounds like it all goes down tomorrow," Kathy spoke softly.

"I guess. Are you worried?"

"Yes."

"Don't be. We've got every angle covered."

"You're not worried?" Kathy questioned.

"I wouldn't say that. I'm nervous, which I think means I'm worried a little."

"You are worried. Just like me. It doesn't matter what other names you call it. It's still worry."

"Okay, I'm worried," Jerry gave in.

"I'm worried for you. I don't want to lose you," Kathy continued to whisper.

"And, I don't want to lose you." They paused to look at each other in the dark. They kissed, but had to make it short. They scanned all the hills and valleys and then made sure the sentinels were still in their location.

"Which shift do you want?" Jerry asked.

"Can you take the first one, because I felt a little distracted when you were out making the call. I need to concentrate. Maybe I'm sleepy."

"Okay, I'll take the first shift. Do you want to go down to the sleeping bags?"

"No, I want to be here with you."

"Okay, here, lean against me. I'll keep you warm." Jerry shifted around so he could scan in all directions but still hold her in his arms. She nestled and became comfortable.

"Jerry?"

"Yes."

"What made you decide to stay a virgin?" Kathy waited.

"Basically, it came from several things, really. My folks talked about how important it was and bragged about how they waited. My older sister didn't wait and got into trouble. That brought a huge pile of lectures from my folks, some of them aimed at me. In high school I wanted to do it, but I had my folk's lectures floating in my head. Then I started dating this girl, and I did and I didn't, you know what I mean?"

Kathy answered with an, "Uh huh." Jerry continued.

"Then the girl I liked suddenly went for another guy and then told everyone I was a virgin. She made it sound like a bad thing. I knew it wasn't bad like she made it out to be. So my response was to make my own mind up about it and stay a virgin until I was married. I got some flak for it from the guys, but after a while it became a part of who I was."

"What was the name of that girl?"

"Cindy."

"Did Cindy ever change her mind about you?"

"No. She eventually married the guy she dumped me for."

"I'm sorry. I'll bet there were plenty of other girls."

"No, nothing serious. A lot of friends, friends who were girls, but not girlfriends. I dated a few here and there. I tried to date in college. There was one in ROTC who seemed nice, but she wasn't interested. I quit ROTC, mostly I had joined because she was there. Then I ran into Sharon. We met a couple of summers ago when I was home working for college money. I remembered her from high school, and we started to date. It seemed like the real thing."

"Did you want to make love with her?"

"Oh, yeah, of course."

"But you didn't."

"No."

"Was she a virgin too?"

"She said she was, but now I don't know. She's back with her old boyfriend." Jerry shrugged and Kathy could feel it.

"I'm sorry you haven't had very good luck with girls," Kathy sympathized.

"I'm lucky now," Jerry whispered and kissed the top of her head. Kathy quietly cooed and worried about the conversation that would eventually come.

"How about you?" Jerry asked. Kathy thought this might be it.

"What do you want to know?"

"I told you about my history. You can tell me about yours." Kathy breathed easier. All she had to do was talk about her past boyfriends.

"Nicky Schmidt was my first big date. He took me to a movie when I was a sophomore. It was the first time I went with a boy in a car just the two of us, no group date with a parent or big sibling driving. I was so excited. We sat and watched the movie, which was this big action war picture he picked out, and we ate popcorn, drank sodas, and he never said a word to me."

"Ooh, not a word?"

"Nope, except for a 'thanks for a nice time' and a scary moment where he leaned in for a kiss."

"Did you kiss him?"

"Are you kidding me? I was so disappointed. I thought it would be nice to talk about each other and share our likes and dislikes. I gave him a hug and a nice thank you."

"So then you never dated again, right?"

"Not exactly. I really wanted to have a nice date, but there were so few boys to choose from in such a small town. Then Ron Eagle Tree, from the Indian reservation, came into my life. He had his own car, and we went many places together. It could have gotten serious, but his folks were not pleased with him dating outside the tribe, because if we got serious, it would jeopardize his chances of becoming tribal chief. I have to explain: his folks were very traditional. They arranged marriages for their children. So…we're still good friends and talk on the phone or e-mail each other from time to time. We made a blood-brother pact only it was a blood-brother-blood-sister pact."

"Was he nice?"

"More than nice. He was a gentleman, fun to talk to, and I thought *then* he was very good looking. He liked to take me horseback riding. That's where I learned to love horses."

"You thought *then* that he was very good looking? What changed your mind?"

"You did."

"Me?"

"Yes, when I met you in the unit at drill weekends, I thought you were a gorgeous hunk, hunkier than hunk," Kathy whispered.

"You must not have seen very many men in your life. I guess that's because you came from a small town," Jerry spoke and then waited for her to catch the jib. Kathy gave him a shove with her body.

"I never dreamed that you and I would be together. I love you so much. You were so handsome and then when you talked me through my disappointment, I fell in love with you deeper than I ever thought possible."

"And you never told me."

"How could I? You were committed to Sharon. I would never break up a couple for my own selfish wants."

"That's my Kathy."

"Thank you. I'm so happy with you." Kathy wanted to keep his warm words as a blanket around her soul.

"Did Al come into the picture after that?" Jerry asked, keeping his voice at a whisper in her ear. This is not where Kathy wanted to go in the conversation.

"Pretty much. There was some dating during my one year at college and then Al—you know all about Al, of course. I must have talked to you about him forever. I'm surprised you weren't bored with it all." She snuggled into his chest, which signaled her desire to get comfortable and sleep.

"When I was with you, I was never bored. Are you comfortable now? Should I go get a sleeping bag?"

"No, please don't move. I'm listening to your heart and feeling you breathe. I've kinda gotten used to that. Goodnight, my Jerry."

"Goodnight, my Kathy."

CHAPTER 10

At the shift change, Jerry left Kathy to watch through the scope while he made a dash down to the sleeping bags. He brought them up and wrapped one around Kathy. She scanned the valley and hillsides with the night scope, catching the usual sightings of nocturnal animals on the move. Jerry wasn't sleepy, but knew sleep was vital to be alert during tomorrow's confrontation. He curled up at Kathy's side, and she persuaded him to lay his head in her lap. This was turning out to be the best guard duty either had experience in the army.

Kathy wanted to let Jerry sleep for a total of two shifts instead of the agreed one. A soldier's sense of duty and team cohesiveness drove her to wake her love, but not before caressing his cheek and whispering her love. Her actions brought him close to awareness. It only took a kiss to complete the task. He sat up and scratched his head.

"Wow, that's the best wake-up call I have ever received from a sergeant."

"Get used to it."

"Anything happening?" Jerry yawned.

"Listen. You can almost hear it. One of those guys is snoring. I wonder if his pal is asleep too?"

"I hear it. Soon the birds will start singing, and that will cover his snoring."

They waited and watched. At the top of the valley, headlights could be seen reflecting on the hills beyond. The lights became stationary and then turned off. About twenty minutes later, forms could be seen moving along hills on both sides of the valley, coming down toward them. The figures were in twos.

"Here they come," Kathy whispered.

"I guess I need to set the grenades in place. I didn't want to do it too soon, but now's the time." Jerry kissed Kathy and slunk down the hill to the mine. After he was completely inside the tunnel, he turned on his headlamp and proceeded with the first grenade. He wedged it into the space between the support beam and the rock ceiling just inside the entrance. At the next support he did the same and the same for the next two. He had one grenade at each of the first four supports. Then, starting from the first, he strung the cord through the pull rings of the first three and tied the end of the cord on to the pull ring of the fourth. Backing up one support he took a small stick and tied it to the cord in front of the ring, repeating the same for the following two. He had all the grenades linked in sequence from one to another. Then he camouflaged the cord by putting it behind old non-functioning electrical wires used for stringing lights when the mine was in full production. He used loose rocks to cover the grenades as they sat atop the beams. Then he strung the line out the mine entrance under the boards, partially blocking the opening, then down to the metal sheet lying flat before the opening.

Returning to Kathy, he whispered, "All set. Now we have to wait for the right time."

"They seem to be framing the valley and moving to elevated vantage points. Soon they'll be able to see us from several directions."

"All right, we need to move down to our staging area. You spike this weapon, and I'll get the one at the other position." At that they each took a stick of gum and started to chew. "I'll meet you down there," Jerry said.

"Good luck." Jerry carefully crawled to the secondary sentinel position. Kathy stayed a moment to chew the gum. Then she took a small portion and skewered it with a finishing nail and drove the wad into the barrel with a small stick. She left the rifle in a position that looked readily available to point and shoot. Then, like Jerry, she low-crawled out of the position and down to a prearranged hiding place below the mine. Jerry joined her a few moments later, having spiked the revolver in the other lookout spot. They were ready.

※※※

Three vehicles drew alongside each other and opened their windows to coordinate.

"Follow me," Webber instructed and drove away. Several miles down the road, he parked amongst some pines. He got out and strapped on his gear with a rucksack full of daily needs. The men gathered in a rough circle.

"All indicators point to them being either in Phantom Canyon or in the valleys to either side. We'll split into teams and move along the ridges on either side, set up at good viewpoints, and wait till we see them move. Bradley and I will be in the middle down by Eight Mile Creek. I'll be able to go either way once we find them. Questions?" Webber asked.

"Sir, do you want us to shoot on sight?"

"Yes, if it looks like they might be getting away. If they're not moving, then call me and we'll plan. If we catch 'em alive, we might be able to persuade them to tell us where the money is. However, in any event, I don't want them to get away. Call me if you're in doubt. Any more questions? …Okay, be careful. They're armed and know how to kill. Don't give away your position. Put your walkie-talkies on minimal sound."

The teams split quietly and zigzagged up the incline to gain the ridges to either side. None spoke. Night scopes were used to peer ahead once they gained the ridge. At intervals they spread out along the high points, watching both sides. When the sun started to light the sky, they were in position.

The pair watched the movements of the teams opposite their hill. Occasionally, they could detect the forms behind and above them. Dark sky, filled with stars, gave way to lighter sky with a few twinkling points of light. They watched as the men settled into their chosen spots. The waiting lasted into the bright morning hours. Kathy and Jerry stayed behind their barricade. Nerves were tense, and neither wanted to talk. At seven in the morning, Kathy spied movement next to the road below. With binoculars she could see two forms stealthily creeping from tree to tree and occasionally stepping on stones at the edge of the creek. After continued watch she pointed and handed the binoculars to Jerry. She whispered, "Bradley and Webber." Jerry nodded in agreement. They watched them as they passed on down to a point about a mile from their position. Two cars came down the road and didn't stop. One drove up the road toward Cripple Creek, stopping occasionally to take pictures of the canyon and the picturesque gold mines that dotted the landscape. Jerry and Kathy did not want civilians caught in any of the action that might transpire.

At nine thirty Jerry made a phone call to Webber. "Got the money?"

"I'm standing in the bank right now, making the last withdrawal."

"Good. Now take it in the two rucksacks and put them in a locker at the bus station. Take the key and put it in an envelope and tape it under the mailbox at the corner of Palmer and Twenty-Sixth Street. It's a nice quiet neighborhood. Do it tonight after midnight."

"I want the video before I do that."

"You're in no position to bargain. But, I will say this. There will be an envelope taped there with some, not all, of the video chips in it as a token of my good favor. After we get the money and are away, free without any harassment from you, then we'll tell you where the last SD chip from the camera can be found. Do we have a deal?"

"Deal."

Jerry hung up. "Not only is he a killer but a good liar as well. I think we shouldn't wait any longer to start." Both took in nervous breaths. They knew it was time to start, but they waited to check every position and to see if there were any civilian cars on the road. It appeared as if the lookouts were still in their respective places. They stared at each other and took several deep breaths to relax their nerves.

"Show time!"

"No, wait! Don't forget to turn off the phone. We don't want any phone calls interrupting our performance," Kathy reminded. Jerry fetched it out of his chest pocket, flipped it open to turn it off, and returned it to its Velcro enclosure.

"Thanks. Okay, now it's show time. Ah, *don't*…break a leg."

The commander again tried to phone Jerry back and listen for the ring tone. He worked the phone to redial when he got a hushed walkie-talkie message from a lookout.

"Commander Webber, I heard a voice to the left and below me," he whispered.

"Where?"

"Below the old mine with the tool shack in front."

"Okay, start moving down. Go left and come down from above them, that will help me see where you are and I can mark your location. Okay, everyone start to close in slowly." Webber began to direct. He didn't need to use the ring tone to locate the pair. This was better because it kept the element of surprise on their side. Two minutes later, he received another call.

"Sir, I found where they slept last night and a thirty-ought-six with a scope. It looks like it was an observation point."

"Good. Bring the rifle with—"

One scream disturbed the calm. It echoed off the canyon wall. Webber couldn't see what some others could see. Kathy was running up the hill toward the mine. She turned and splashed water on Jerry who ran through the water to tackle her at the waist, knocking her down. He then proceeded to undo her shirt by unzipping the front. Kathy kicked him off and began to run. Jerry held on to the jacket-shirt while Kathy raced up the hill, leaving the shirt behind in Jerry's hands. She yelled, "You can have me if you can catch me!" She was in a beige T-shirt, and Jerry was closing the distance. Kathy took off her T-shirt and threw it into the air. Jerry caught it, and just as she was entering the mine, she had her hands behind her back, grabbing at her bra. Jerry hustled in behind her.

Walkie-talkies crackled with competing messages. Webber had to sort through the static. "One at a time! George, What did you see?"

"Sir, I saw them playing."

"Where did they go?"

"To the mine. They went in the entrance to the mine."

"Are you absolutely sure?"

"Yes," George answered.

"I had a clear view, too. I saw them go into the mine. Looks like they're having a lot of fun. They must not suspect anything," Mike cut in.

"Okay, everyone close on the mine, quickly. George, check the hillside, see if there is any other escape route."

The teams hustled to reach the mine. Ted and Gary arrived there first, with the 30-0-6, five minutes after the order to close fast. They took defensive positions ten yards out with weapons pointed at the entrance. More minutes ticked by as others arrived and hid behind the edge of the shack and around the rocks and trees to either side. Webber puffed up the hill and slowly edged into the entrance to peer into the dark. He could tell it was deep.

He backed up and waited for the others to arrive. He made his plan of attack. First he spoke to Bradley.

"I need you to cover any possible avenue of escape. Take this and set up over there." Webber handed him the high-powered rifle with the scope and the box of cartridges after taking it from Ted. "I want you to watch for any escape routes. We don't know if this mine has other exits. If you see them, shoot them. Got it?"

"I want to be there when you kill them. Not sitting on some dumb hill!"

"Do as you are ordered," Webber commanded. "If we catch them, we'll call you in so you won't miss it, okay? If they do have another exit, you are our best tracker, and if you can, shoot them. Here are the keys to my SUV in case you need them. Now go!" Webber watched Bradley go back down the hill; then he turned to the others. "We are going in after them. Ted, Gary, you go in first. Quietly. Use your scopes. If you see them, click once on your WTs and we'll follow. If you need help, click twice and we'll send in another. You can commo with him and he'll return to tell us what you need. You must be very quiet."

The two men entered the mine carefully, weapons at the ready. They were gone about two minutes and a double click came back. Webber signaled in the third man, who entered and returned.

"The mine splits, and we need to cover two branches," the messenger explained. Webber signaled in two more, and the time wore on. Again there was a double click. Webber sent in another two with instructions for one to stand in between and relay messages. The word came back that there was a deep shaft going downward with boards across. Then another messenger came out to report a dead end to the second tunnel. Nerves were starting to run up blood pressure readings of those waiting. Then a message came back.

"Sir, we can hear them. They're having sex. We can hear her." At that report, he sent everyone in except a guard outside and a messenger twenty yards inside. The plan was to use the WTs when they could freely communicate. Webber would say when.

Inside the entrance, Jerry handed Kathy her T-shirt. "You put a little more into the act than what was planned. I didn't expect you to take your T-shirt off."

"I wanted it to be realistic."

"Nice touch! Maybe we should have thought of dropping some clothing along this mineshaft. Oh, well. Next time." Jerry turned and ran down the tunnel, putting on his headlamp. Kathy redressed and slipped into the drain and low crawled out the door, behind the log and debris they had placed there, and to the metal sheet. She lifted it and placed a sizeable rock under the edge. She rolled under and into one of the shallow graves. She made herself as comfortable as possible. Jerry completed his run down to the planks, avoiding the sound alarms. He used a remote for the CD player to turn it on. He hid the remote and ran back up to the entrance. He too slid into the drain and crawled to the sheet of corrugated metal, rolled under, and pushed the rock out, lowering the metal to the ground. The graves were dug with one connection, a place in which to hold hands. They waited with guns drawn.

Soon there was some shuffling, then quiet, then more shuffling and some panting from those who had come uphill. They heard the instructions Webber gave Bradley. Jerry could not see Kathy's eyes, but he gave her a reassuring squeeze with his hand. When the plan of attack was made, a couple of the men stood on the rusted corrugated sheet. It brought tension to the two below. They listened. Each moment built more anxiety into the next. It felt like it had taken forever for Webber to take the bait. They heard the crunch of footsteps on the gravel as the men moved into the mine. Jerry worried that the few flashlights and scopes would cause some to return. However, the lure of catching their prey with their pants down dominated thoughts.

Both soldiers had weapons at the ready. Jerry had the end of the cord leading to the grenades. He gave them five long enervating minutes, listened to see where the guard might be, and then gently pulled in on the cord. Slack line amounted to about two feet. The cord came into his hand all dusty and dirty from the dirt spread over the top to conceal it on the ground. Then he felt a little resistance; he tugged gently, and it came forward another six inches. They could hear the tinkle of the grenade release-spoons as they fell to the floor. The guard was intrigued by the sound and stuck his head in the entrance. There was a slight split second lead to the first explosion over the other three. Dirt, rock, boards, and a body flew out of the opening, landing on the sheet of metal and spewing rocks over the side of the mountain. Thick dust ascended into the sky. When it eventually cleared there was a sunken rectangle traveling up the mountain from where the entrance of the mine had been.

Their ears were ringing. Usually on the grenade range they would have been wearing ear protection. They neglected that point. Jerry had seen the shadow of the guard approach the entrance at the point of explosion but didn't know for sure what may have happened to him. He pushed up on the metal and found it to be much heavier. He grunted, and Kathy heard and tried to help. They pushed and heaved. Some of the d'êtres shifted off the edge of the sheet, causing it to be a little lighter. They struggled until Jerry could worm his way out of the grave and between the ground and the metal. He edged sideways and finally poked his head out into the opening, then an arm, and finally his chest. With his arm he brushed more trash off and managed to slip out. He saw the heaps of rock and the body on top. He dragged it off and rolled more stones off. On his knees, he lifted the opposite edge, and got Kathy out. They looked at the dead body first and then the mine. It was a pile of sunken rubble.

"Next time we do this, we make our hideout farther away," she rasped quietly, her throat caked with dust. "Bradley's out there somewhere. We need to avoid him." They slunk to the ground to move behind the shack and down to their former hideout. The dust was beginning to clear.

Bradley jumped, almost dropping the rifle. He didn't know what to do. His commander was in the mine. He hadn't seen any other exit and no movement, dust concealed everything in the area. There was no detectable movement around the shack or the place where the entrance used to be. *Are they all dead?* He thought it had to be some kind of accident that had killed or trapped everyone inside. He debated his course of action. He decided to try to help and left his vantage point to approach the destroyed mine. He slung the rifle over his shoulder and ran down the hill and ran back up the next. He was in reasonable shape, but still felt the exertion of running up an incline after witnessing a blast that may have killed his nearest associates. He did not see the two soldiers hiding to his right as he scrambled by them. He reached the shack and found the body crumpled at the edge of the rusted metal sheet. He attacked the rock rubble where the entry used to be.

Frantically he worked at digging his way to an opening. With the running and excavating, his hands and body rebelled and told him to sit. He sat with his head down, defeated. Looking at the ground, he could see the marks of traffic on the dust. Footprints were here and there, mingled with knee imprints. He lifted the edge of the metal, finding the indentations where the soldiers had hidden. Instantly he seized the rifle and moved to an open area where he could view the valley. He watched. He almost stopped his surveillance in favor of tracking the couple when he saw their movement through the trees on the opposite side of the valley. He dropped to his belly, wrapped the sling twice around his arm and began to sight for the best possible spot where they would be exposed. He found little. They were carefully using the foliage to hide their escape. He waited.

Near the top of the ridge, there were some broken areas of the greenery, and he hoped they would reveal themselves there. It was difficult to spot them in their Army combat uniforms. The only advantage he had was to watch for movement. Then he saw them. He led their movement by a small margin and squeezed the trigger. The bullet slammed into the nail in the barrel and with no other place to go it broke through the side of the barrel and fragmented to the left. Bradley was injured on the side of his face with small fragments radiating backward. He was not badly wounded, mostly mad. He took out his nine millimeter and fired angrily at the far hill, spraying the hillside with bullets.

Pockets of loose rock tumbled to the floor from walls and ceilings, timbers used for support work fell over and in places portions of the roof fell in. The posse members had been knocked to the ground by the explosions. Ears vibrated, stinging the brain. It was a full minute before some started to move and sounds could be vaguely heard. They stood knocking gravel and dust off their clothes, their mission momentarily forgotten. Webber tried to clear his ears. He shook his head. After repeated attempts, subtle sounds came to him, and then he heard the giggling and laughter of the soldiers further into the mine. *How could they still be having…* The truth struck him full in his gut. He staggered forward past several men and hastened down the tunnel. He went past the CD player and then came back to find it tucked into the rock behind the beam. It was still playing. He was so angry he struck the player, knocking it to the ground. It still played. Kathy's voice could clearly be heard saying, "Oh, I like that. More!" Webber kicked the player, sending it down the tunnel. "More." One of Webber's men had mercy on the commander and hit the stop button.

They stood in silence, putting together what had been done to them. They had been tricked. As if stadium lights had been turn on, and had given them the same thought, all in one accord rushed back toward the entrance to find rubble blocking their egress. The relay messenger who had been stationed near the entrance and who had sounded an alarm lay on the ground partially covered in stone; he was wounded in the back but was alive. They dug him out and listened to him explain that he had heard and saw the grenade pins and spoons dropping and had run to avoid getting killed. Webber ordered first aid for the man and tried to collect his thoughts. He tried to communicate outside the mine with both his WT and his cell phone. He only had communication with those standing near him as he heard his own voice through their WTs. He wondered how the two could be seen coming in but not going out. He ordered his men to explore the mine and find the soldiers or find the second exit. He told them to be on their guard, weapons ready.

Five minutes later one of his men radioed. "Sir, you need to see this."

"Where are you?"

"Just past the CD player about fifteen yards or so."

"On my way."

The commander advanced around the slight turn to the tunnel and found three of his men in a loose gaggle, looking at the pile of supplies: cases of water bottles, canned goods, flash lights, and extra batteries. A handwritten sign sat on top. It read,

You might be here for a while. This food and water may come in handy. Don't forget to thank a veteran for your freedom!

Webber emitted an expletive and kicked the nearest stack. An envelope slipped to the floor. Intrigued, he picked it up to see several photographs Jerry had printed of him pointing his revolver at a man in the hole. He threw the pictures down in disgust.

"Where are the other men?" He didn't ask if they had found another exit, he knew the answer to that already. He stomped back up the tunnel to meet the others who had descended the downward shaft. They explained the shaft and its various tunnels leading to dead ends. Webber assigned men in shifts of two to begin work on removing debris from the entrance.

They ran down the ridge to a plateau and skirted Mitre Peak. They knew that as soon as Bradley was to his vehicle he would backtrack a couple of miles north and then come screaming down Golden Park Valley. If he came down Phantom Canyon, it would take longer with all the twisting turns. They hoped but did not believe in the best-case scenario of Bradley taking the slower direction. They knew he had seen them going due west.

They ran. At one point they leapt off a small bluff and slid on their sides, feet first, down a steep gravel slope. They were not covering their tracks, as it was more than apparent where they had gone.

Upon reaching the truck, they climbed in and made haste down the dusty gravel road. They had planned this to be a leisurely drive into town. Instead, they were attempting to get away and get lost in the traffic. Cañon City was not a metropolis. It consisted of a number of large residential areas on the edges of one main road, which was a state highway leading into the mountains from the prairie thirty miles to the east. They didn't want a high-speed chase through town, as it would alert the police, putting them on the hunt as well. They pushed the little truck to its limit as it exited the valley and drove across the wide-open ranch land as it bordered the town.

Jerry felt the sluggishness in the turns and then could feel the pull to the left when he was on a straightaway. A front tire was going flat. Kathy was busy staring back at the road behind them.

"I think we're getting a flat tire," Jerry said in a deflated tone.

"What? This never happens in the movies. The good guys never get a flat tire! We *are* the good guys aren't we? What're we going to do?"

"Change it of course. Keep a watch on the road behind." Jerry edged to the side of the road, stopping on flat ground. Taking off his jacket-shirt, he wrestled the seat back, got the lug wrench and jack out, and proceeded to ratchet the front end of the truck up. Kathy popped the hubcap off and applied the wrench to the nuts until she had the right size. She couldn't budge the nut. Jerry finished lifting the truck and took the wrench from Kathy, applying everything he had. Kathy went to the back of the truck to get the tire out from beneath the bed. Nervously, she looked up the road and saw a plume of road dust mounting up from behind an oncoming car in the distance.

"Jerry, what're we going to do? There's no place to hide out there." Kathy pointed to the open fields on either side of the road. There was a thoughtful moment before Jerry acted. He started taking off his pants. "This is *not* the time to go swimming, Jerry." She sounded a bit exasperated.

"I need to change my clothes. Help me." He stuffed his army pants in the cab of the truck as Kathy threw him his pants and shirt. He left his shirt hanging out on one side. "I need your hat." Without question, she tossed him her floppy hat. He ripped it and then rubbed it in the dirt. "Kathy, lay down in the cab outta sight. Have your weapon ready just in case." Kathy slipped into the cab but watched Jerry complete his disguise. Jerry cast around for a stick and assumed a position by the front wheel. While he waited, he managed to get one lug nut loosened and applied the wrench to another. The speeding SUV approached, and Jerry rose from the wheel and assumed a bent position leaning on the stick. Kathy got a glimpse of Jerry. He looked like a tired old man with a tattered hat, hunched shoulders, and about to fall over.

Kathy saw Bradley approach at top speed. When she looked at Jerry, she saw an old man feebly step out into the road to wave for help with a flat tire. She ducked down and heard Bradley accelerate and rush by. Jerry doddered further into the road and continued to wave at the receding SUV and then took baby steps back to the pickup. He leaned on the window. He looked at Kathy who had an appearance of respect for his quick thinking.

"You know, these last few days have taken a lot out of me. I suddenly feel fifty years older," Jerry quipped.

"I love you, no matter how much older you are than me." Kathy kissed him through the window. "You owe me a hat!"

They recommenced changing the tire, but left the truck up on its jack. Jerry explained. "If we fix this and leave right away, Bradley may come back and know something's up. He's probably searching the roads in town for which way we might have gone. If we were to return back up the valley, he could follow. I suggest we wait it out here for a while." They climbed into the cab and sat waiting. If they needed to, they could start the engine and drive off the jack. They waited.

"This is not like the movies. Usually the get-a-way people are trying to get away!" Kathy observed.

"Two good guys sitting in a jacked up truck on the side of the road doesn't make for exciting action drama."

"How long do you think we should wait?"

"How long do you think Bradley will be screaming around town trying to find us before he gives up?"

"I don't know. It's a small town…half an hour. Maybe he'll set up on the edge of town and watch for us," Kathy calculated.

"So maybe we should head back up the road to Cripple Creek and get out and down to Colorado Springs that way."

"Good Idea. I'm going to change while we wait." Kathy used the open door of the truck to shield her from possible oncoming cars. Jerry respectfully kept his eyes forward as she slipped out of her uniform and into the jeans and shirt she had worn the day before. "So, that's how you keep from being intimate with women. You don't look at disrobed women?"

"It helps."

"For someone of your persuasion, you sure know how to write a sexy script, though." Kathy teased.

"I have an imagination, but I didn't write the part about you ripping your T-shirt off in front of an audience. That was your ad-lib."

"Are you jealous about me doing that in front of them?"

"A little."

"Really? Look at it this way. It looks the same as a white bikini. And from a distance they probably didn't get a very good look anyway."

"A white lacy bikini," Jerry said matter-of-factly.

"Ahh, so you noticed," Kathy answered with a smile.

"How could I not notice? You're gorgeous!"

"Thank you. That's nice." Kathy settled into his comfortable compliment. Then she thought about another line of thought. "So, Mr. How-Could-I-Not-Notice, what kind of swimsuit would you like to see me in?"

"A bikini."

"Do you mean a two piece or a real bikini?" Kathy asked with curiosity.

"A real one with those strings tying it together."

Kathy had a moment to think about it then asked, "What color?"

"White…with lace."

"I can see I'll need to get a good tan."

"Do you think it might be time to go?" Jerry asked.

"We could risk it. I hate going back into the mountains with him on the prowl."

"Let's drive real slow. When we get to Cripple Creek, we can stop there and hide, or drive on down to the Springs. We still have some work to get done." Jerry slipped out of the cab, lowered the front end, and put the jack back behind the seat. They did a U-turn and slowly drove up the road, trying not to raise any dust. Kathy watched for cars coming from behind. When they got into the valley behind concealing foliage, Jerry hit the pedal and flew up the mountain gorge. They stayed on the highway and then came down into the city from the west.

They were relieved to check into a hotel downtown and get the materials out of storage. They typed up the conclusion to the narration of events and printed out copies. They added the extra pages to each of the packages and went to the post office, sending off all but several packages—one for Det. Soriano, several more just in case. They went to the restaurant across from Starbucks and took a table up on the balcony. Kathy ordered while Jerry went across the street to Starbucks.

Soriano was at home getting ready to have dinner with his wife. His cell rang, and he walked into his study when he saw that it was coming from a pay phone.

"Hello, Det. Soriano, I'm sorry to keep you waiting for my next call. We've been a little busy. I have a package for you."

"Let me guess. The package contains pictures and videos."

"Yes, sir, and a description of all the events from beginning to end. It also includes a marked map where you can find the body of the murdered undercover agent and where you can find Officer Webber and some of his posse."

"Are they having some kind of a meeting?"

"Sort of. They're in an old gold mine that has collapsed. They're trapped and need help getting out, that is, if the mine didn't totally collapse on them. I suggest you look at the video first and then mount a rescue attempt, making sure you bring enough deputies to make the arrests. Oh, and be aware there's a dead posse member out in front of the mine. He ended up being in the wrong place at the wrong time."

Det. Soriano groaned at the news. "I'm guessing you aren't going to hand the package to me in person."

"I'll leave it at the Starbucks where we first met. I wouldn't wait very long to get it, some people might get curious."

"Okay, I'll leave now and come for it. Ah, Sgt. Svenson, I checked out your stories, yours and Sgt. Pelletier's. They make a lot of sense. The details you guys gave me were right on. However, it would be helpful if I had Det. Probasco's service revolver. It might help to prove his complicity in your abduction. Can you tell me where it is?"

"Yes, sir, I cleaned it off and threw it out the window onto a rocky slope just before you get to the Broadmoor Hotel. I hope it helps you. I'll talk to you later sometime. Please be careful." Jerry hung up. He left the package with the barista, explaining that he had to go and his friend was coming by in a few minutes to pick it up. He left a nice tip and walked out, down the street, and up the other side to return to the balcony with Kathy. Their orders had arrived, and they ate.

Twenty minutes later they watched Soriano enter the coffee shop and emerge with the package. He paused, looking up and down the street, then across the street and up at the balcony. He looked directly at the pair. He saw them and lifted the package in the air in salute. They were just about to race out the back, when Soriano went to his car and left. Uneasy, they finished the last few bites and paid for the meal and left.

At a downtown hotel, they washed off the effects of the last thirty-six hours. Kathy went first and then Jerry. He found her lounging in her long nightshirt on the bed with a towel on her head maharaja style. He had on a shirt and clean pants, which attracted her attention.

"Are you going out?"

"I was thinking that we didn't get dessert. Would you like to come with me on a date? It would be our first official date." Kathy didn't answer. She scrambled off the bed in a hurry and then spun around in confusion. "What should I wear? I don't have anything to wear."

"Anything you wear would be special because you're in it," Jerry complimented.

"But my hair, my hair is wet!"

"We're not in a rush. We have lots of time. I'll sit here and watch my Kathy turn inside out."

"Ooh, you're such a dear." She kissed him on the lips. "Shoes, I don't have any shoes, just these hiking boots. I'm going to look a mess!"

Jerry laughed. "I was planning on walking the few blocks to Michelle's Ice Cream Parlor, but we can drive to a Walmart. They stay open late."

"Would you please? I can't look like a frump on our first date."

"Don't worry, I already know you're beautiful." Kathy did not hear Jerry's words because she had the bathroom hairdryer on full blast.

They had on their disguises with wigs. They drove to the nearest Walmart, and Kathy insisted Jerry remain in the truck. She went in alone and came out forty minutes later. She had on a simple red A-line dress with a string of white pearls around her neck. She had matching shoes and a purse. She had obviously worked her wig, in the bathroom, to complete the look. All her clothes plus hiking boots were in plastic sales bags. Jerry got out and opened the passenger side door for her to enter.

"Now, I look like a frump compared to you, especially with this goofy long hair," Jerry answered.

"No you don't, you always look handsome."

"I tried that line on you, and it didn't work."

"When I use it on you, it will always work, because it's true." She winked.

"When I said it, it was true."

"That's different. I'm a woman."

"I can't argue with that."

※❈❈

It was close to sundown when Soriano and the teams of police officers and laborers arrived at the mineshaft. They found the body and put forensics on the task of securing the area around the entrance. Soriano felt they could start removing rubble from the caved-in area above the entrance. They set up floodlights and worked around the clock excavating into the sunken area. Soriano had the county sheriff at his side directing the operation and who wanted to know the instant a breakthrough was achieved. Tomorrow they also planned to exhume the body that the video and the map had indicated. It would be a long night, but both were determined to be there the moment they could see Lieutenant Webber emerge and the look on his face when he was arrested.

After two in the morning, an increase in activity indicated a new development. More clustered around the digging. Then there was a guarded shout that they had broken through. Police officers gathered closer. The first survivor stepped out looking in better shape than the men who were doing the shoveling and prying of stones out of the hole. One by one they emerged. Each was taken to a separate area, arrested, cuffed, and led away to a cruiser. Then the wounded man was handed out. Lastly, Lieutenant Webber stepped out into the cool morning air. Without preamble they cuffed him and read him his rights.

Bradley reached the second commander on the phone. He related the entire story. The new commander listened and instructed Bradley to hide; he needed to get Bradley out of the area.

They chose to keep the truck hidden in covered hotel parking and walk the short distance to Michelle's. They sat in a corner booth with the front door visible to Jerry. He had a banana split, and she had a double chocolate strawberry sundae. They savored the treats after so many months of army food. Kathy possessed a happy, almost forget-everything-else demeanor. She was on a date, a date with the right man, her man. Jerry enjoyed observing her playful mood. He took a small piece of paper out of his pocket, rolling and folding it over and over again.

"What's that you have in your hand?" Kathy asked. Jerry didn't answer her question immediately.

"I have a suggestion."

"What about?"

"We've talked about having to change our identities. I think we should choose names before we make false IDs."

"Did you have anything in mind?" Kathy warmed to the subject.

"I'm not very good at making up first names. I was wondering if you could pick out a first name for me and a first name for you?"

"That's interesting. You want me to pick your name?"

"Yes, but don't pick an old name; pick one that's a little more modern, something that you would really like. And then I'm sure you have thought of names you might have wanted your mom and dad to name you. Something you would like to hear me call you."

"I'll have to think about that a little. What about last names? Sometimes first names sound better with a good last name."

"I planned on throwing out a suggestion."

"Okay, tell me what you've got." Kathy was into this adventure. Jerry hesitated a moment for a bit of drama and then he handed her the folded paper. Kathy opened and read the writing.

Mr. And Mrs. Shuster

"Ooh, Jerry, my Jerry! Is this your way of saying you want me to be your wife?" Kathy's eyes were filling up. Jerry took both her hands in his.

"Kathy, my Kathy, will you be my wife…forever?"

"Yes, of course…forever." Kathy knew she had to tell him, but now was not the time. This was a moment to be cherished for all time. She could talk about serious things later. Jerry got out of his side of the booth and slipped in beside her. They locked into an embrace and kissed for what seemed like hours. Customers around them sensed something momentous. They watched and waited to ask what had happened, but never caught the couple's eye. They were in their own world. After the embrace they had their foreheads almost touching as they looked into each other's eyes.

"Did you pick Shuster for a reason?" Kathy whispered.

"In honor of Corporal Shuster who we knew. He was so young. He deserved to live, have a wife, and kids. I think it might be a way for him to live on a little in our lives. We could carry his last name."

"That's beautiful, Jerry. I like your sentiment. I would be proud to be your Mrs. Shuster."

"What do you think of the name Devin?" Kathy asked.

"Devin… ummm, Devin. For me or for you?" Jerry quipped. Kathy gave him a little shove.

"Do you like it?" she asked.

"Yeah, I think so. I've never thought about the name, but it has a certain quality to it. Devin? …Devin! Deeevin. It works. Why did you choose this name?"

"I read it in a story many years ago when I was a girl, and I thought it would be a nice name if I had a baby boy."

"Okay, I accept Devin. Now what do you want me to call you?"

"When I was young, I sometimes made up names for myself: Mia, Sophia, Rachel. I favored one at one time and then another at another time."

"Which one do you see yourself being now?" Jerry asked, and Kathy closed her eyes to imagine.

"Mr. and Mrs. Devin, and Mia Shuster. I think that goes together for me. What about you?" Jerry nodded his head and smiled. He could see she was in another dimension. "This is fun!" She held his head in her hands and applied another kiss. They never saw the watching faces from the other tables and booths.

"Jerry, where are we going to live? Where are we going to raise a family? So you can go camping with them like you planned."

"I have a plan." Jerry got quiet and looked around.

"What is it?" Kathy was almost jumping out of her seat.

"Well, first I want you to veto it if you don't like it or change it to make it better if you want to."

"Okay."

"We can't live in the United States. The posse could be anywhere, seeking us out. We change our names, and then we go to a foreign country."

"Which country?" Kathy questioned.

"I did some checking on the Internet while you were busy in the shower. There's a country that is known for its banking system and it is remote enough for us to live peacefully; the banking would be for investments for charity and for us to live off of. Does that sound all right to you?"

"Yes, it does. Living anywhere with you would be fine with me. Where is it?"

"How about Antarctica?" Jerry tried to look serious.

"Antarctica does not have a banking system. It doesn't have a bank! Now tell me the truth...No, wait, let me guess."

"You want to guess? There are a lot of countries."

"It'll be fun to guess. Be prepared for a lot of guesses. I already have two clues. How hard can it be? Just promise me you'll say yes when I get it." Kathy liked the game.

"You're on!" Jerry challenged.

"Switzerland."

"Ah...no."

"It's known for its banking, and it's beautiful."

"Nice try, but still no."

"Jerry, I mean, Devin, we have a lot of planning to do. Where we are going to get married, when and...everything? Oh, what about the honeymoon? Where are we going to go?"

"Slow down, one thing at a time. I do have a plan for that too."

"What? Tell me, tell me!" Kathy still couldn't stop her bubbling enthusiasm.

Jerry got quieter. "We still have to be careful. We can't make big open moves. I think a perfect place to hide is on the open sea. Let's take a cruise."

"Yes! A long one. Relaxing and comfortable with lots of warm sun."

"You're dreaming again."

"I am, in a perfect dream with you in it. I love it and I really love you. This is the best first date I have ever had. How are you going to top this one?"

"By being married to you." They kissed again. When they stopped they looked around. Faces were turned on them and made them feel conspicuous. Jerry checked the rest of the shop to find an officer at the counter giving his order. They were trapped in the back of the parlor. They whispered and waited. The officer got his cone and took a seat at a small table. If they left, they would have to walk by him. They waited. They play-acted their former conversation before Jerry had made his proposal. Nerves replaced glee. Their conditional happiness depended on their escape to a different world. Sobering reality forced itself upon the happy moment.

It took ten minutes for the policeman to finish and amble out. They waited another ten and exited. Their eyes were darting everywhere as they walked back to their hotel. They took a longer path that meandered around several blocks. They vowed to get out of town to where their faces were not as well known.

In the room, Kathy shot into high gear again asking about and planning for the wedding. She didn't have to be reminded that it would have to be small and inauspicious. Then she stopped abruptly. She got serious and Jerry saw the transformation.

"What's wrong, my Kathy?"

"We need to talk."

"What about?"

"About me."

"What could there be about you that could make you suddenly change into a pile of worry. I can see it in your face."

"Devin, I'm not like you."

"That's for sure. You're gorgeous and beautiful and witty. You are everything I could ask for."

"Thank you, but that's not my point. I'm embarrassed and ashamed. I'm afraid to tell you."

"What could it be, Sweetheart?"

"Devin, I'm not like you because I'm not a virgin. I wish I was. I wish for all the world I could give you the gift you're giving me. Sadly, I gave it away to a man I loved, who I thought really loved me. I wish I could change that and have you be my only one. I feel awful. I'm not what you are. I don't deserve you." Kathy was close to tears. She was hoping for his approval, but he was quiet. She waited for his answer and the more the seconds ticked by, the more she feared the worst. He began slowly.

"Mia, a person I highly respect said to me once, 'Just remember I won't be jealous. The present and the future is what I want. Everything that has happened to you in the past makes you the nice person you are today.' I liked the wisdom of those words. They meant a lot to me then and they can mean a lot to you now." Jerry extended both hands out to her and she took them. He pulled her up from the chair and he wrapped strong arms around her. She was dropping tears on her dress.

"I said those words to you and you remembered them. Do you really mean it?" she asked.

"Yes, I do." Jerry lifted her chin, wet with tears and kissed her eyes. "I will love you always from the present to the future," he promised. They embraced for several minutes.

"Thank you."

"Are you always going to thank me every time we kiss?" Jerry asked.

"I should, I suppose, but I'm thanking you for being you. You are more than I dreamed."

CHAPTER 11

The next morning was filled with preparation. Kathy called her minister from her hometown and arranged a date suitable for him at a restaurant outside of her hometown. She called her brother and asked him to arrange an outing with their folks to the restaurant for an evening meal. She asked him to sneak into the folks' attic and get her mother's wedding dress. He was proud to be a part of her surprise plan and got the whole family and her other brothers to help. He would be the best man.

Jerry's folks had to be cajoled into driving a hundred miles to meet for dinner. He told them it was important and they finally agreed. It was after he told them he would be dropping out of the Army reserves, which did the trick. He got his sister on the line and asked her to be the maid of honor without letting the folks in on the surprise. Everything was going to be a family affair with no outsiders.

They drove to inner city Denver and walked the shabby streets in an undesirable neighborhood. They asked various individuals for someone who could make some IDs for them. A homeless man with a shopping cart finally knew of someone who might know where they could go. Tracking down the information took several conversations punctuated with hundred dollar bills. They found a back door entrance to a wooden stairway leading to a private photo lab. It cost them eight thousand in cash to get false driver's licenses and passports. They needed full names.

"Got any ideas for our middle names?" Jerry asked.

"Yes, Gerald and Kathleen. That way we can still call each other 'my Jerry' and 'my Kathy.'"

"I like it," Jerry pronounced. It took an hour for good quality workmanship. They paid the fee and were back on the road south to Colorado Springs.

Then they executed their deception plan with the money left over in their bank accounts. They rounded up homeless and paid for them to stay in various motels for the night. They used their debit cards. When they had put a dozen homeless into a dozen motels they left the cards with the last recipients, asking them to get food and new clothing with the remainder. The police would have a nightmare tracking down all the rooms trying to find them while they drove out of town toward South Dakota.

❈

The old pick-up had a bench seat. Mia sat next to Devin in the middle, just like in the sixties. They enjoyed every mile, every vista, and every bump in the road. Their eyes were glassy with love. The more they traveled, the safer they felt.

"Canada?"

"No."

"Mexico?"

"No, besides we would have to learn another language," Devin explained.

"Oh, good another clue. Where we are going they speak English."

"I think so. I'm not sure."

"Now you're just being difficult," Mia protested.

"Not really; I didn't think of the language problem until you mentioned Mexico. But, language wouldn't be too problematic. International banking is always in English," Devin answered.

"Devin, we're almost there. I'm so excited. My parents are going to be so surprised tomorrow night."

"Mine too."

"Where are we going to stay? This is a small town," Kathy asked.

"Let's find a place away from town, maybe near the interstate and work out of there."

"Okay… England. What about England? They speak English there."

"Nope."

"Australia?"

"Too far."

"Can we ever be too far from the posse?"

"I hope so, but I wasn't thinking about Australia. I wouldn't think of English speaking places if I were you, it's limiting your guesses."

"Okay. Brazil?"

"Nope."

⁂

When Kathy and Jerry, alias Mia and Devin, entered the restaurant, they stopped conversations at every table. She was dressed in a flowing white bridal gown with pearls sewed to the fabric in the old fashion style. He had rented a tux in basic black with a large black bow tie. They walked to the reserved banquet room past customers who smiled at the happy couple. The minister was already there. He wanted to work the sequence of events before anybody arrived. He congratulated the bride and groom and told of how he had known Kathy since she was the girl who played with his daughter and they had gone to school together. He did a quick rundown and then indulged in idle talk until family members started to arrive.

Mia's other brothers came first and started the happy back-slapping and handshaking with the groom. They referred to themselves as Kathy and Jerry. Their false personas would come later. Kisses on cheeks were exchanged so as not to ruin the bride's make-up. Whispers from sisters-in-laws were exchanged, usually telling her how handsome her man was and how beautiful she looked.

Then Jerry's folks arrived. They were all smiles, but not surprised. Jerry was hugged and congratulated.

"Dad, Mom, you don't seem surprised."

"We kind of figured it out when your sister insisted on wearing a formal dress. Our questions broke her down to where she had to confess she was the maid of honor. Gerald, don't worry. We are so happy for you. Introduce us to your bride." They exchanged pleasantries. Mrs. Svenson had tears in her eyes.

Then there was a hush as Kathy's brother opened the door to allow her dad to enter. He wheeled the chair between the jambs and concentrated on not scratching the door. Mrs. Pelletier followed with her cane. Both discovered the surprise at the same moment when they raised their eyes upon fully entering the room.

"Katherine, is that you?" Her voice wavered.

"Yes, mother, it's me."

"You're getting married? Tonight? Right now?" Mrs. Pelletier was adding the information as it came to her eyes. "In my dress?" At that she looked at her oldest and said, "So that's why you were up in the attic!" And then back to Kathy. "Does it fit?"

Kathy decided to get to the hugging instead of answering all the questions her mother was already answering all by herself. They embraced, exchanged words of happiness, and never mentioned the worries they had about the circumstances of the past few days. They were more than curious about Kathy's man and wanted to get as much information as possible without prying. The two families merged in the joyous event. It was a long time before the minister could start the proceedings.

Applause and cheers were the happy response of the observers when the couple was pronounced man and wife. They walked around the family members and beamed with glee. Jerry turned to the one waiter standing by the door and nodded. Then announced.

"Dinner is on us." They gathered at a long table decorated with candles and cherub centerpieces. The food was ready and waiting and the toasts started in earnest. The happy couple sat across from both parents. Kathy took an opportunity to rise and come around behind Jerry's folks. She whispered in their ears.

"I want you to know that Jerry followed your advice about sex before marriage. You did a wonderful job of raising him! " She endeared herself to the Svensons.

"Have you already started with the family secrets, sis?" her older brother chided when he saw the whispering communication.

"Yep," Kathy said without giving the least hint that she would tell.

"Okay then can you tell us where you're going on your honeymoon," he asked.

"That's not a family secret." Kathy paused. "That's a couple's secret!" She kissed her brother's cheek and went to each of her bothers and did the same. She had a good sit down talk fest with Jerry's sisters. Kathy hardly ate a thing; she flitted from one group to another. They had ordered a cake for dessert and cut huge slices for everyone. The evening hours transpired into night hours and the restaurant was near closing. The minister signed the marriage documents as well as the witnesses. Jerry said they had been in such a rush they hadn't time to fill in their own names. They would do that later and send it in. That's when they gave each of their parents a package containing the story and the video. They told the folks it would be comforting to know that their children were innocent no matter what might be said about them. The packages were only for the families, not to be shared around the community for fear of retributions from possible posse members in the area.

The bill for the evening dinner was prepaid. They tipped the wait staff. And as they walked outside, they made promises to stay in contact. After they performed a round robin of hugs and repeated congratulations, they walked toward the cars. Jerry put

Kathy in, started the engine, and began slowly driving away with tin cans and streamers following. Kathy realized that having Colorado license plates was a dead give away to her brothers. The noise could be heard for hundreds of yards in every direction.

⧉

The drive southeast started the next morning with two grinning and happy occupants. They planned on driving during the daylight because they didn't want to get stopped by policemen reminding them they had a taillight out. They were in a hurry to get to Florida and catch a cruise. For about ten miles Mia quizzed Devin about possible countries and then she changed the rules of the game.

"I'll never guess it with about a million countries out there to choose from. You have to let me narrow down the search area."

"Okay. I'll be kind."

"Western Hemisphere?"

"Yes."

"South America?"

"No."

"Central America?"

"Sort a."

"I got it! The Caribbean."

"Yes."

"Oh, Devin, you're trying to make my dream come true. I love you! Bahamas?"

"No."

"Barbuda?"

"No."

They played and teased each other all the way to the port of Miami. There they opened a bank account in their new names and gave away the trusty pickup. They shopped for new outfits for their new persona. Then they checked onto the ship and took a leisurely sail to various ports. They did not finish the cruise because they got off at Nassau and hired private boats to island-hop until they reached the Turks and Caicos Islands.

They settled into a manor house on the beach on one of the many picturesque islands and started their investment for charity operation. They built a stable for horses and bought a fast boat for fishing and a quick get-away, if needed.

EPILOGUE

L ying on the sand with water gently caressing her feet lay a suntanned beauty in a white string bikini. Around one wrist was the rein of a beautiful black stallion taking a breather from a gallop down the sandy beach. In tropical long shorts, her blond-haired husband approached.

"My Kathy, are you dreaming again?"

"No, this is reality. You made my dreams come true, now I'm working on your dream."

"My dream? What dream would that be?"

"You know the one where you get to go camping with the kids and watch them poke sticks in the fire?"

"Oh, that dream. I don't see us camping right now and no campfire. How are you working on my dream?"

"I'm busy making the first child."

"Are you…ah, you know?"

"Yes, I am, my Jerry. I'm expecting our first."